"So you swam out here to capture a sea siren?"

Renie couldn't believe it. Dave had caught her as a mermaid!

"Mermaids can take human form in all the stories," Dave said. That's why he'd had to swim out to her rock, to see if she really. . . "Usually they play cruel tricks on mortals. Are you one of those who plays cruel tricks?"

"I guess you'll just have to take your chances." She ran her fingers along his thigh and drew closer to him on the rock. "In the legends, mermaids must seduce men." She offered herself to his embrace.

Dave smoothed her hair back so he could feel her bare breasts against his chest. His hands moved gently over her shoulders, then over her breasts as he kissed her. Renie trembled in his arms.

She was his fantasy. The fantasy of all men. She was a love-starved siren with primal urges that had to be satisfied. Had to be obeyed. She was enchantment. She was danger. . . .

Dave couldn't resist her.

Prolific and popular **Regan Forest** is the author of nine Temptation romances. Wildly imaginative, Regan likes to put her characters into unusual situations. "What if," she wondered, "a man saw a mermaid, and then he fell in love with her in her human form?" She created a hero with his own tortured past, and the story unfolded. A resident of Tucson, Arizona, Regan is a full-time writer. Don't miss her next Temptation romance, a wonderful time-travel story, available soon.

Books by Regan Forest

HARLEQUIN TEMPTATION
152–WHEREVER LOVE LEADS
176–A WANTED MAN
216–WHEN TOMORROW COMES
226–HEAVEN SENT
311–HIDDEN MESSAGES
355–THE LADY AND THE DRAGON

Secret Lives

REGAN FOREST

Harlequin Books

TORONTO • NEW YORK • LONDON
AMSTERDAM • PARIS • SYDNEY • HAMBURG
STOCKHOLM • ATHENS • TOKYO • MILAN
MADRID • WARSAW • BUDAPEST • AUCKLAND

For Jane, with love

Published June 1992

ISBN 0-373-25499-7

SECRET LIVES

Printed in U.S.A.

Prologue

WHEN HIS FLIGHT NUMBER is called, an Englishman named David Collister lines up, presents his boarding pass, and starts through the jetway. Halfway down the tunnel, a fiery pain shoots through his stomach, a pain so sharp he doubles over. Two chattering women behind him walk squarely into him, a child trips over the women, topples and begins to howl. The whole line of passengers halts to see what the screaming is about.

In the ensuing confusion, Collister stumbles sideways in a panic. The pain is debilitating, and he is headed for the deep bush of Africa, where medical facilities are few. He doesn't dare get onto the plane with the ulcer giving him such agony.

Perspiring, he slides away from the noisy pileup he has caused, and pushes his way back clutching a locked briefcase containing £ 380,000. The airline representative who is collecting boarding passes has moved from her post, too distracted by the disturbance in the tunnel to notice him reenter the terminal.

To those turbulent, half-blind seconds, David Collister owes his life, but he has no way of knowing that the seconds of pain that save him are also the end of life as he knows it.

1

LOOKING DOWN from the rocks above the unnamed cove in the blue of twilight, Dave suddenly sat forward. On one of the tiny islets below he saw a mermaid.

He closed his eyes in disbelief and opened them again, expecting the illusion to be gone. The creature was still there; a woman with the tail of a fish! Her waist-length hair, wet from the sea, flowed over her shoulders, partially concealing full, naked breasts. The iridescent fishtail reflected the colors of the sunset, its filmy, silvery fins shivering in the pale pink light.

Eyes fixed steadily on what had to be an apparition, Dave gripped a jut of rock so tightly that the jagged edge cut into his hand and made it bleed. He held on, as if convinced that with enough pain he would wake from whatever dream he had fallen into, or be released from the macabre tricks his eyes were playing on him.

The pain changed nothing. There was no mistaking what he saw. He tried to make the figure human, but she was not. Unaware of the blood from his hand that was spilling onto the rock, he sat dead still and watched her. In a few moments the mermaid moved her arms, as if stretching, slid down the lichen-covered rock and disappeared into the sea.

Dave tried to follow her path, but shadows were moving in the waves, and soon he could see only the swells of dark blue water on the surface of the sea.

He glanced down at the blood without really seeing it. *This creature is a biological impossibility!* he argued. Mammal and fish? Warm and cold blood? Skin and scales? Lungs and gills? No such creature could exist, and yet he had seen one, just as many sailors in sea legends had done.

He knew the stories—the fairy tales. Illusions.

This illusion, though, was so real it left him trembling. As twilight turned to darkness around him, he stared at the mysterious sea shadows and knew what he had seen.

And yet . . .

Had he been in the South of France too long . . . hiding too long? Had his own life grown so unreal that he could no longer distinguish reality from fantasy?

Hell, had he written one fantasy story too many? Had some hard surface of reality cracked open and let him fall through?

Half of Dave—the part that wrote stories in order to earn a living—believed in such things as magic and mermaids. The other half—the practical side that ached to stop dodging the law and return to England—knew better.

With daylight almost gone, he climbed back up the slope. Wild herbs crushed under his shoes sent perfumes into the night air—incense for magic spells.

The village of Cauvier sat perched on a hillside above the sea, little changed from medieval times. Now, as then, its winding, narrow streets were stirring with evening signs; workers coming from the fields, shop-keepers closing for the day, children playing. From open windows came aromas of cooking. Normally the smells of tomato and garlic would have whetted Dave's appetite. Tonight all he wanted was a drink.

At the fountain in the village square he held his cut hand under splashing water. The bleeding had stopped. Under the street lamp he examined the jagged wound, angry with himself because it hurt.

His mates would be expecting him at the bar that had been on the corner of the town square for three hundred years. Seldom during those years had its door been closed. It stood open now, as always. Inside, the wooden floors were worn gray. One wall was mirrored, reflecting the length of the bar and the tables along the side of the narrow room. A corner alcove displayed challenge cups won by the establishment's teams of *boules* players.

Dave paused in the doorway. Edwin Noble was here, as usual, playing cards at the corner table. Edwin greeted his fellow countryman in French. The two British expatriates never spoke English unless they were alone, and sometimes not even then. After two years in the South of France, Dave did not always think in English anymore.

A large brown dog sleeping beside the table opened his eyes and raised his eyebrows. Dave greeted the animal by name and sat down.

"There is blood on your pants," his friend Émile said. "And your eyes look glazed. What's the matter with you?"

"I cut myself climbing on the rocks. It's nothing." He took a paper serviette from the table and wrapped it around the cut on his palm.

He ordered *pastis* and addressed Jean-Claude, the oldest man in the group. "So, my friend, have you been fishing today?"

"I fish every day," the old man answered, brushing his white mustache with his fingertips. His suntanned skin was like worn leather, his eyes were half-closed. By this time of day he would have been in the bar for two hours or more.

Dave's drink came—Pernod over ice in a glass, served with a pitcher of water. Dave watched the liquid turn from clear to milky as he mixed it, then he gulped down half. Strangely, the fragrances of the herbs on the hillside lingered in his mind like the perfume of a woman he had touched. As if he were bewitched. The sight of a mermaid bewitched poor mortals; the stories always said so.

He set down his glass, wiped his mouth with the back of his hand and looked at the old man. "You've been around this coast longer than any of us, Pépère. You know the local legends. The children sometimes tell stories of sea monsters and mermaids. You've been at sea all your life. How many mermaids have you seen?"

Dave was surprised to see the older man's dark eyes grow somber. Jean-Claude answered slowly, "I haven't seen a mermaid personally. But my grandfather saw one when he was a young man. He told the story many times. One summer twilight, as he was heading back from the open sea, he saw her on an islet. When she saw the boat approaching, she slid into the water."

"Where was this? Where on the coast?"

"Leeward from the unnamed cove, off the coast from the white sand. In those days there was a fishing pier there. Some years later, because of the tourists, the pier was moved to where it is now."

Edwin Noble set his cards down and looked at the old man with British skepticism. "Hang on, Pépère. You say your grandfather saw a live mermaid? How did he describe the thing?"

"He wasn't close enough to see her facial features, but she had long yellow hair, skin like mother-of-pearl and a tail of silver and gold."

"Your old granddad must have nipped at his bottle early that day," said Émile with a laugh.

Except for squinting at him, Jean-Claude ignored the sarcasm. "To see a mermaid is bad luck. My grandfather's luck turned very bad after that."

Dave Andrews glanced at the makeshift bandage on his palm, drops of blood had trickled through the paper serviette. The hand was bleeding again. Every seaman knew mermaids were omens of bad luck. He hadn't thought of that until now.

Edwin Noble scratched his head and grinned. "Mermaids sing, you know. Sweet songs foretelling impending disaster."

"Sweet songs of lust," Dave remembered, drinking steadily now. "If a mermaid sets her sights on a mortal man, she'll stop at nothing to ensnare him in order to satisfy her carnal lust."

"That's right." Émile grinned. "That's the way it is in all the stories. Insatiable lust. If they set their sights on a seaman, he is doomed."

Edwin Noble laughed. "Carnal lust?" He gathered up the cards and began to shuffle the deck. "May I point out that mermaids have a certain curious handicap?"

"Perhaps that's why the lust is insatiable," Émile chortled, knocking Dave on the shoulder.

Dave held up his glass to order another *pastis*. "Has anyone else around here ever seen a mermaid?" His tone was mild, but his heart was beating faster; he believed what he had seen in the cove. Believed without believing.

"There was Count Raymond," Émile said. "Count Raymond was married to a mermaid called Mélusine. Mind you, the count had no idea his wife was a mermaid, but once a week Mélusine had to take on her true form, so she forbade him to see her on that day. Raymond promised and then broke his word and discovered her secret. Mélusine fled, and since then her cries can be heard near the sea to foretell death."

"That's only a fable," Dave objected. "Unreliable. I meant something more recent."

The other men looked at each other and shook their heads.

"Why is it important?" Edwin asked.

Dave rubbed the stubble of his beard and looked from one man to the other. "Because I believe Jean-Claude's grandfather was a smart and sober man."

"*Oui,*" Jean-Claude agreed. "All those years ago, before the whole of Europe darkened our summer coast like flocks of screaming birds, there was a mermaid here. I am sure she is gone now."

"We can't count on that," Edwin said, lighting a cig-arette. "Mermaids live for centuries. Right, Davey, lad? Could it be you've seen her?"

Dave gazed at his companions through the smoky air. He waited for Victor, the waiter, to set his drink up on the table. "Of course I have," he answered finally. "I'm simply curious as to whether I'm the only one."

The group burst into laughter. The old dog raised his head as if to say, "There's someone trying to sleep here, in case you fellows hadn't noticed."

Edwin Noble blew a cloud of smoke into the stale air. "And did you hear her singing?"

"I heard nothing."

"That was lucky," Jean-Claude answered, his mus-tache twitching. "If you had heard her singing you would be doomed."

Nodding, Émile warned, "Mermaids are clever. They can take on human form to lure a mortal. If she saw you she will want you." He studied the cards he had just been dealt. "You are a strong and handsome lad. If she saw you, the sea creature will find you again, *mon ami.*"

EARLY the following morning, his hand still throbbing whenever he grasped anything solid, Dave Andrews, whose name in his native England had been David Collister, climbed the rocks again above the Mediter-ranean coast, a pair of high-powered binoculars dan-gling over his shoulder.

The sun rose like a fireball out of the sapphire sea. Behind him loomed the high, red cliffs and hillsides of pine, some of which had been blackened by last year's fires. The morning was freshened by a hint of autumn and the hope of rain again after the summer drought.

Last night's foolery in the bar had scrambled his mind. Bad luck, they'd said. Bad luck to experience so beautiful an illusion? A creature who lives in the depths of the sea and rises only to find and capture love? Dave smiled. It was daylight now and the sea was calm. A few fishing boats and pleasure crafts were out. A familiar yacht was anchored near the mouth of the cove.

Before twenty minutes had passed, he had convinced himself there was nothing below the surf but the fish that belonged there.

Still, because he was a man who trusted his senses, Dave found last night's vision interfering with his work throughout that day . . . the vision of shining, wet hair, the ample breasts, the graceful movement of her arms as she stretched. Had he seen only her upper torso, he would have believed she was a local girl out for an evening swim. But he had clearly seen all of her, and the bottom half was fish.

Twilight, the time he had seen her yesterday, found him out there again on the ledge, scanning the cove with binoculars. He saw ripples in the water by the islet and then, to his amazement, she was there, hoisting herself from the water onto the flat, lichen-covered rock.

She pulled herself up until she could swing the cumbersome tail around and use it for support. Once on the rock, she stretched and lay down on her back, arms under her head, as if watching the sky and waiting for the night's first stars to appear. She breathed heavily, like a swimmer out of breath.

A classic beauty with delicate features, this was the most exquisite female face he had ever seen. Her long, thick hair sparkled as if held by an invisible net of pearls. Her eyelashes fluttered, long and dark. Her skin was the color of pale seashells. Her bare breasts, shining wet, looked translucent, as touchable as alabaster.

Dave's heart pumped wildly. Every nerve in his body tingled as though a thousand needles were pricking him. His hands reluctantly eased the focus of his binoculars down the length of her body.

Shot through with an unwelcome chill—the kind that accompanies dread—he forced himself to face what the lenses brought close. Candescent scales like those of a fish grew from her skin in a thin layer over her lower abdomen. The scales thickened over her thighs and pelvis and formed a tail. The appendage was narrow and filmy, silver-blue fins on each side and a wide, silver caudal fin. The soft rainbow colors of the scales reflected lights from the rays of the setting sun like ten thousand tiny, twinkling prisms.

Dave felt dizzy, and cold, tingling sensations assaulted his nervous system. He was at once enchanted, repelled, exhilarated and tormented.

Why him?

A strange, windless silence descended. Above the eternal groaning of the waves he imagined he heard her humming. He could not shake a haunting feeling that she knew he was on the shore, watching her.

Mermaids were lonely in the sea, the legends claimed. They surfaced from the depths of their murky water world to seek love . . . but never found it. . . .

The bright-hued glow of sunset was blending into the sea, changing the azure water to the color of sapphires. The mermaid stirred and stretched, lifting her slim, white arms toward the sky as if in some strange ritual. Again she slid back into the sea.

Not once had she turned to look in the direction of the shore. Would she not be curious about it? he wondered. Would she not be fascinated by the sea's edge, the forested mountains and the lights flickering up and down the coast like clusters of spilled stars? Would she not ponder the mysteries of the land of the mortals?

Or had she been here?

THAT NIGHT the patrons of the little bar in the village square did not see him. This was not unusual, for the young *Anglais* was elusive by nature. He knew the villagers gossiped about him eagerly because they knew nothing of his life before Provence. Their questions brought only stares from his cold blue eyes, they would shrink back into the shadows of his silence, and a new story would take root. He knew that when he wasn't in the bar they talked about him. He was the foreigner who'd paid cash for the house on the town's highest hill and who could not possibly make enough money repairing boat engines to live as he did. The villagers, including his regular drinking companions, were curious about who he really was.

They would never know.

What Dave had witnessed today in the unnamed cove he would share with no one, either. Not tonight, not ever. Sitting alone in the silence of his room, he thought of her and was overcome by loneliness. It was a new kind; it gnawed into the core of his soul, deeper than all the accumulated loneliness of his exile.

During the last two interminable years in France, he had resisted thinking about being forever alone. But now he did, and all because he had seen a face even more beautiful than those of the mermaids in the books of his childhood.

Maybe he ought to accept the fact that the sight of a mermaid meant bad luck. With this awful surge of loneliness tonight, it was starting already.

Loneliness was like pain first hitting his heart, then his stomach. The damned ulcer again. Dave closed his eyes. The pain always forced his mind back to that day.... The pain always made him remember....

Heathrow Airport. The swarthy face of a man at the boarding gate . . . a man with shifting eyes and two fingers missing from his right hand. I observe the man without curiosity as he sits facing me from an opposite row of plastic airport chairs. We are passengers waiting to board the same flight to Zimbabwe.

I look up from my newspaper for a moment to see a second passenger enter the departure lounge, establish eye contact with the swarthy-faced man, and then disappear.

Minutes later, after ducking back out of the jetway and into the terminal, perspiring with pain, I swallow a handful of pills without benefit of water, and slide onto a chair, waiting for the worst of the pain to subside. By the time it does, it is of no concern to me that the door to my flight is closed.

The pain is all that matters.

The face of my fellow passenger with the missing fingers is unimportant, already forgotten.

Until later. A long time later, on the French Riviera, in exile. When I remember, it is too late.

2

DAVE FELT A SNEEZE coming on while he was carrying a full cup of tea from the kitchen to his study. In a panic, he tried to make it to the first available table without spilling the tea. At that precise moment his white bull terrier, Morgan, spotted a tennis ball under a chair and made a headlong dive.

Sneezing violently, Dave tripped over the dog. The tea splashed like a fountain over his shirt, desk, computer and Morgan's startled face.

The dog dropped the ball and licked his nose, looking up at his master as if to say, "What did you do that for, you clumsy oaf?"

Dave pulled his shirt over his head and began mopping at the computer with the part of the fabric that was still dry. "Thanks, man's best friend," he muttered sourly. "You and that bloody ball."

Wagging his tail happily, Morgan, having realized he liked the taste of the sweetened liquid, assisted by licking the floor, the edge of the desk and the wet papers stacked there.

There was no hope of salvaging those papers; they would have to be reprinted. Dave sneezed again. "I'm probably allergic to dog!"

Tail still wagging, Morgan picked up the ball, interpreting the insults as a friendly morning chat. Dave returned to the kitchen for a fresh cup of tea.

Then again, he thought, finally settling at his desk, maybe it was dust that had made him sneeze. The dust of last spring and summer lay like a fine mist over this cluttered room. A hermit's room.

The Wizard's room, where *The Wizard's Fireside Tales* took form, his own magical tales of fantasy for children. Dave had never intended to become the Wizard. In his exile he had begun dabbling in fantasy stories, the kind he'd read as a lad, the kind he had always had some secret yearning to create himself. And he had stumbled onto a viable source of income.

The unique style and charismatic characters of his strange read-to stories had been in demand since his first story had been published. Even now, when the books had become a popular series, his publisher still did not know his real name. As far as the world knew, David Collister had died in a plane crash two years ago.

Dave turned on his computer and watched the screen words come to life like little green ghosts stepping out of the night. Last night Fireskog, the hairy goblin with two fingers missing from his right hand, had been hot on the trail of the Wandering Prince of Lost Clouds. The Wandering Prince was in grave danger from his archenemy, Fireskog, because an invisible net of Neptune's enchantment had rendered him helpless. Last night the half elf prince had seen a mermaid rise out of the World under the Waves and been temporarily blinded by her beauty.

For ten minutes Dave stared at the monitor, feeling numb. His eyes wandered restlessly to the sunlit window, from which he could overlook the red tile roofs of the village and the church tower, and hear the bell that rang every morning and evening with the rising and the setting of the sun. Beyond, past rust-hued rocks garnished with pine shrubs and splashes of wildflowers, was the sea; the beach of Savenay and to the north, the unnamed cove, where he had seen her.

He could think of nothing but the mermaid.

His gaze moved back to the screen. Remembering her golden hair, he named her Silka...Princess of the Deep, a tantalizing seductress who would make the Wandering Prince fall helplessly in love. In her watery realm the Prince would think he was safe from the goblins Fireskog and Grig, but the poor, bumbling prince would be wrong. As usual.

Dave wrote, deleted, sketched the mermaid on a notepad and wrote again, until he gave in to overwhelming restlessness. This morning it was driving him crazy to mix thoughts of the mermaid with his memories of the three-fingered man at Heathrow. A murderer. His hairy goblin, hideous though he was, was no competition for human evil. Fireskog was merely an outlet for Dave's frustration.

Creating Silka was another escape hatch. She existed, too, although she couldn't. Maybe he was going mad.

Frustrated, he gulped the last of the tepid sea and flipped off the monitor; the Wizard's world disappeared, and the dark screen reflected smoky images of his own movements. The ghost of himself. He rose, kicking the chair back with enough force to topple it. The sleeping dog jumped in alarm.

"I'm going to the marina," he said to Morgan, flexing his hand to test the pain from the healing cut on his palm. A small bandage would keep out engine grease.

Word had spread around the village that Dave was good at repairing boat engines. At first he'd taken on the jobs because he needed the money. Now he needed the challenge of physical labor. Yesterday Sébastien Fabre had tracked Dave down with a complaint that his cruiser engine was overheating. Dave had promised to have a look at it today.

The bull terrier stood, ball in mouth, wagging his tail expectantly. His little eyes were pleading.

"All right, you can go. But you will stay with me and not run off to the bar to start a fight with Bertrand under the table. Understand? One more dogfight with Bertrand and you will be permanently banned from the village square. Are you listening, Morg? You'll stay with me on the boat deck. You can't get into mischief on the boat deck."

So Dave thought. He should have known better.

HE STEPPED ABOARD and grabbed the lines to pull the boat close enough to the catwalk for his dog to reach the deck. Morgan did not relish jumping over water.

The terrier trotted about the new territory, sniffing the life jackets and fishing equipment, exploring every corner, while his master got to work on the engine.

Dave diagnosed the problem as a clogged cooling system. The pump was all but ruined. He would need to persuade Sébastien that a new pressure gauge ought to be installed.

A sudden, loud commotion roused him. Ferocious barking and the shrieking howls of a cat. In the cramped confines of the engine hatch, Dave banged his head against the gear pump and climbed out, swearing. Morgan had pushed the hatch door open, wandered into the cabin and found a cat.

A white, half-grown kitten, with Morgan racing after it, streaked across the deck in terror, bounded over the rail and onto the catwalk. The dog jumped up and down against the bulkhead, screaming hysterically.

Sébastien's pet was getting away. Dave leaped off the deck and tore after it, knowing he had no chance in hell of catching a frightened kitten. The little animal ran up the catwalk and onto the main pier.

Into the reaching arms of a woman who was walking up from the sea end of the dock.

Grunting with relief, Dave halted. The woman, wearing a wide-brimmed hat, was dressed all in white; white slacks, white blouse, a chiffon sash of silver blue around her slender waist. She held the kitten against her chest, looking down at it. He could see only white on white. Her ringless hands were slender and as pale as the pearls that hung around the kitten's little head. The crown of her brimmed hat was sheer; through it he could see the shine of golden hair. A long blond braid fell over one shoulder.

"*Merci!* You don't know how glad I am that you were here!" he said in French, over the sounds of crazed barking and gnashing coming from the boat deck.

She raised her head and smiled at him.

Dave reeled, frozen. He might have been zapped by a current of live electricity, the shock was so strong. That face! It was the face of the mermaid!

His heart pounded like a drum. It was her! The powerful lens of his binoculars had brought her face as close as it was now. He forced his staring eyes from her face to her legs. Legs. Under well-fitting white slacks were *legs*.

He had gone over the edge and landed in madness. *Count Raymond's mermaid wife took human form. All mermaids could take human form. They set their lustful sights on unsuspecting mortals. . . .*

The woman said nothing, only smiled and stroked the kitten, trying to calm it. Tufts of soft white fur against pale, gentle fingers. Morgan's absurd howling was making the frightened cat struggle. Dave fought to get his voice back, struggling uselessly to deny the realization that was overpowering him: this was the most beautiful woman he had ever seen. *And she was not human.*

The cat sensed something, too. It suddenly calmed and snuggled against her breast. Dave held up his grease-blackened hands to take the little white feline from its rescuer, and muttered awkwardly in French, "I apologize for the engine grease. . . ." He wiped his palms against the seat of his jeans.

Still she stood in silence, looking at him with mysterious, sea-blue eyes. Her eyes, like her pale lips, were smiling. She was not offering to hand over the cat; she seemed to rather enjoy cuddling it.

"My . . . dog's behavior is inexcusable," he said apologetically, embarrassed by Morgan's screaming and very ill at ease with the woman's silence.

Their eyes met. *"Je ne parle . . . pas français,"* she said haltingly.

This threw him. If she didn't speak French, what *did* she speak?

"English?" he asked doubtfully, wondering if she would smile again.

"Oh, thank God! Somebody around here speaks English!"

His mouth fell open. "You sound American!"

She laughed, ruffling the kitten's fur. "Is that so astonishing?"

"I just . . . hadn't thought . . ."

"What were you saying in French?" she asked.

"I was apologizing for the noise my dog is making."

"He must be vicious!"

"Not in the least. Just self-centered and immature and wildly jealous of any member of the feline race."

"You're English," she said. "Is this your boat?"

"No, it belongs to a friend. I was just working on the engine. I live in Cauvier." He pointed to the mountain. "The village that hangs on the side of the hill."

She squinted into the sun. "It looks lovely."

"Are you on holiday?" he asked.

"Not really. I . . ." She hesitated, then finished, "Well, yes, I guess you could say that."

Not the straight answer one would expect from a simple question. Her American accent was perfect. Talk about someone leading a double life!

He held out his hand. "My name is Dave Andrews."

"Renée Lloyd." She looked down at the kitten. "And your friend?"

"A resident of the boat. I didn't even know she was on board until Morgan invaded the cabin. Morgan is the howler over there. He looks like a bull terrier, but in actual fact he is a criminal in a dog suit."

"You can't put this poor frightened kitty back on the boat with Morgan."

"No," he agreed. "But I can disembark Morgan. We'll coordinate this."

"Okay." She followed him down the catwalk and waited while he jumped aboard and pulled in the boat, close enough for Morgan, with a boost of his rear end, to leap onto the wooden walk. At that moment the woman handed the kitten across to Dave.

It scurried for the safety of the cabin.

Renée Lloyd stood in a sea of growls, the dog's tail slapping against her leg. Muttering apologies again, Dave stepped off the cruiser. Subdued by his master's **grim** expression, Morgan followed them onto the pier and ran down the dock in search of some new form of entertainment.

"Thanks for the help," Dave said.

"My pleasure."

"Renée," he said softly, trying her name for the first time.

"Everyone calls me Renie. When I was a kid and got my first typewriter, I discovered the keyboard had no accent mark for my name. So I changed my name to Renie and it stuck."

He gazed at her. "You had a typewriter?"

She gazed back, the blue eyes sparkling. "Don't most people?"

He shrugged. *How in hell could she have legs today on the pier and a fishtail yesterday in the sea?* When mermaids disguised themselves as mortals, they were scheming to trap a man. All mariners knew that. Dave's imagination spun out of control. But her beauty held him.

His curiosity was so powerful that he knew he would do anything he had to do to keep her from getting away.

He asked, "Were you coming in from a boat just now?"

"Yes, from the harbor taxi. We're sitting at anchor out near the cove."

"We?"

"My niece and I."

"Your niece."

"Yes."

Dave swallowed. There were two of them, and one a child. He had noticed a large cruiser anchored at the mouth of the cove. In fact he knew the boat, the *Sandrine II*. It was one of several that was regularly leased to tourists.

He said, "I'm thirsty. By chance are you free to join me for an aperitif?"

"I'd like to. It's great to find somebody who speaks English."

He smiled, feeling shaky, wondering if he was doing the right thing. But he couldn't help himself. He had to find out if what was happening was real or a dream. "I'll have to go aboard and put the cover back on the engine hatch and clean up. Would you mind waiting?"

"Of course not."

Once aboard, he took her hand and helped her onto the deck. "Make yourself comfortable. I won't be long."

She sat down on the fantail cushions under the shade of the tarpaulin awning, watching with interest. He lowered himself to the engine bed to take another look at the connection between the cooling system and the water pump, trying to estimate what he would need for a pressure gauge installation, but his brain was only half functioning.

Quickly he hauled himself out of the hatch and went below to wash his hands and face. The white kitten was nowhere in sight.

When he came back up, the woman was still there and still real. She was leaning against the cushions, gazing up at the sky.

"What are you looking at?"

"Oh!" she said. "Dave, look at this! A sunbow!"

To the west, centered in a nest of white clouds, was a bright circle of colors.

"A sun dog," he said. "Sailors believe they're an omen."

She shaded her eyes, looking fascinated. "What kind of omen?"

"I don't remember."

"But is it good or bad?"

He shook his head, wishing he *could* remember.

She smiled. "I declare it a good omen, then. Sailors are so superstitious, aren't they? You came back on deck just in time. It's disappearing."

They watched until the circle of color had faded into the white of the clouds.

"There is a small café across the street," he said. "If you don't mind my greasy clothes, we can walk over there."

"Sure. Let's go. Where has your dog disappeared to, by the way?"

"He likes to root around the dock pilings at low tide. He'll find me. If not, he knows where my car is parked. Morgan always looks out for himself."

At the café table he asked, "What would you like to drink?"

"Wine would be nice. What's the best kind to order?"

"*Vin du pays*," he answered. "One of the local wines. Or maybe you'd like what we call *vin blanc cassis*, which is a white wine mixed with blackcurrant liqueur. It's quite good, actually."

"Okay. Sounds nice. Will you have it, too?"

"Why not?"

He gave the order and sat gazing across the table at eyes the color of blue sky reflected on water...light blue eyes almost exactly the color of his own. She wore pale pink lipstick and pearl earrings that matched the string of pearls around her neck. Of course, pearls, gemstones of the sea. On the French Riviera women rarely wore clothes, but she wore a long-sleeved blouse and a brimmed hat.

"How long are you staying on the Côte d'Azur?" he asked, when their drinks had come.

"I'm not sure. Hopefully for some weeks."

"And then?"

"I don't know yet, for sure."

"But somewhere near the ocean," he prodded.

"Oh, yes, near a warm ocean. And what about you, Dave Andrews? Why did you leave England?"

"I couldn't stand the English winters anymore," he lied and wondered about her.

She was amazing. She seemed so much like an ordinary woman—clothes, jewelry, flowery perfume that he got a whiff of now and then. She leased a yacht and anchored it at the cove instead of its regular slip at the marina basin, and then had to take a motorboat back and forth. He knew why she preferred to stay on the open sea—at night she became a fish.

Trying to picture a smaller version of a woman-fish, he asked, "Where is your niece now?"

"Gods knows. The last I saw of her she was heading for the beach with a bottle of wine in one hand and a French-English dictionary in the other."

"A bottle of wine?"

Renie laughed. "Were you picturing a child? Twila is a year older than me. I just happen to have a brother who is twenty-two years my senior, and he married young."

"I . . . uh . . . I see."

She grinned. "You look puzzled. It's not all that unusual."

"You have a brother?"

He knew he sounded like a parrot, but was unable to take in what he was hearing. If he had not seen this lady sitting out on a damn rock, flapping an enormous tail . . . But he *had* seen her out there.

"I have two brothers," she replied. "Do you? Have a brother?"

"No. Well, a stepbrother. Not the same thing." Dave shifted uncomfortably. He hated the subject of families because he missed his family sometimes.

Would her brother be a merman? Where was the crossover into the realm of magic? How the bloody hell did it happen? He gulped the drink in front of him and ordered another.

Renie looked at her watch.

"Are you late?" he asked.

"A little. I came in to do some shopping before I hunt down my renegade niece to remind her we have...plans for the late afternoon."

"Perhaps you haven't seen much of the Riviera," he began. "If you like, we could take a drive tomorrow. I could show you about."

"Terrific! I'd love it! What time?"

The pearls at her neck shone against the silk of her blouse. He was imagining her long hair unbraided and flowing, the way he had seen it last night....

"Dave?"

"Uh...lunchtime," he answered. "I have a favorite little bistro some kilometers up the coast, where we can have lunch. Its speciality is seafood."

"Seafood is my favorite. I'll look forward to it. I'll meet you here at the marina. One o'clock?"

He nodded and accepted her extended hand.

"You have another drink coming." She smiled. "Don't get up."

He rose with her. "Can I drop you somewhere?"

"No. I'm off to the local shops. Thanks for the aperitif."

Suddenly she seemed in a hurry. He watched her make her way around the tables.

Turning back, she smiled at him again. "That sun dog was a good omen, you know!"

When he could no longer see her, Dave sat staring into the dark purple drink, seeing black, ominous circles. Sun dogs were not good omens, he remembered.

Mermaids were not good omens, either. They foretold doom. They were creatures with an insatiable lust who captured mortal men in their nets. . . .

And did *what* with the men they wanted to seduce? Did *what*?

Let's find out what.

He poked a finger into his glass to dissolve the gray-black rainbows before he drank. In reality, he thought, mermaids were *not* beautiful women; they were creatures of the Otherworld.

In reality? What reality? There *was* no reality!

Dave thought of her beauty and gave up fighting the illusion. He had tripped and fallen into a realm beyond logic, a realm where every rule was different and every moment a vaporous thing that could disappear if he dared to close his eyes too long.

3

THE CURRENTS WERE STRONG between the islet and the anchored yacht, and the sea became heavier as it grew deeper near the mouth of the cove. The last half of the swim took too much of her strength. The fishtail propelled her, but its weight had to be compensated for. Her arms ached with the effort, and her back felt stiff.

After what seemed an hour, she reached the yacht and grabbed the sides of the rope loop that dangled from the afterdeck. The boat rocked against its anchor lines. Waves lapped at the hull. Their gentle slapping was the only sound to break the night silence of the open sea.

"Twila!" she called. "Are you up there?"

In the dim light a face appeared over the railing. "What took you so long? You're twenty-five minutes overdue."

"I needed time to rest." Moving the cumbersome fishtail, Renie managed to balance herself in a sitting position on the swing. "Okay, I'm on! Crank me in."

The small motor of the makeshift swing whirred, and she was lifted up the side of the white hull. Twila pulled the swing forward and immediately wrapped a beach towel around Renie's bare shoulders.

Renie coiled the thick towel around her while she squirmed off the pulley and onto a pile of orange canvas deck cushions, her tail flapping awkwardly.

"An inebriated seal moves more gracefully than you out of water," Twila said, producing a second towel.

Vigorously towel-drying her long, blond hair, Renie smiled. "Sometime—some other time—you must tell me how you happened to know how an inebriated seal behaves."

"You don't want to know. How'd you do out there?"

"Better than yesterday. But this is proving more difficult than I figured. Especially when the waves rise. I lost more strength when I was hurt than I realized."

The other woman knelt beside her. She touched the sharp scales of the fishtail, which, still wet from the sea, shone silver and gold in the light of the deck lamps. "You'll do it, Auntie Ren. I have absolute faith in you. I do think you're pushing the late hour, though. It's dark. You shouldn't be swimming in the ocean in the dark."

"As long as I can still see even a little, I'm just fine. Good Lord, Twila, you wouldn't want me to risk being spotted by someone."

"By whom? We're too far out. Nobody's out here. No other boats."

Renie reached for another dry towel and wrapped it turban style around her hair. She stretched her body on the canvas deck cushions, flapping the fishtail. "Come on. I'm starving and exhausted. Help me out of this damn thing."

Getting her out was a painstaking process, because the fishtail was all but molded to her body. Custom-made, it was tight enough to protect her like a wet suit; her skin was dry underneath. This was a necessary part of the design, to keep her legs from getting cold. Velcro fasteners were concealed under the scales, but even unzipped at the top, it took the two of them, struggling, to peel the thing off her body like an outer layer of skin; carefully, so as not to damage the paper-thin, metallic scales.

Freed of her costume, Renie hurried down the steps to the cabin and the shower.

Some minutes later she emerged, dressed in jeans and a sweatshirt, drying her long hair. Twila was in the galley boiling a pot of pasta. "Dinner is almost ready, Charlie Tuna."

Renie headed up the wooden steps to the deck. "Great. I'll be down as soon as I tuck my tail in for the night."

On deck once again, she hosed down the scaly costume with fresh water from the ship's tanks before laying it carefully upon flat cushions inside the wheelhouse. When the job was done, she turned out all the deck lights except the required night signals, red on port, green on starboard. Darkness as soft as velvet fell around her. The Mediterranean breeze was balmy, and the boat rocked in the gentle waves.

Standing at the starboard rail, Renie looked at the lights on shore. It was dark behind the unnamed cove, but a bit farther south, down the coast, shone the lights of civilization. And on the a hillside that rose steeply skyward were sprinkles of lights from the medieval village where Dave Andrews lived.

To the sparkling lights of the coast she said, "Who would ever have thought I'd wind up on the French Riviera . . . and as a fish, of all things?"

The aroma of freshly brewed coffee lured her from the boat railing into the warm cabin again. The wood-paneled saloon was small and cozy. Splendid maintenance showed on every inch of the thirty-year-old craft, unusual for one that was rented. It's original brass fittings were polished. Red- and yellow-cushioned bunks lined the bulkhead on two sides. Above, a narrow, glass-doored locker held a collection of books and maps of Provence and the Côte d'Azur, all printed in French. A drop-leaf table separated the saloon from the galley.

Twila had the table set for a meal of spaghetti, bread with garlic butter and a salad of lettuce, mushrooms and tomatoes. She was pouring coffee. "Bryan What's-his-name called on the ship's phone. He's somewhere around Saint-Raphael, scouting film sites. He wanted to know how you were doing. I told him you were in the sea learning to breathe like a carp. He replied, naturally, that it was damned late for you to be in the sea, and I told him not to worry because my spunky Auntie Renie felt as secure out there as any other fish. Which he is free to interpret any way he chooses, since fish aren't generally your most secure individuals on the planet. He'll be in touch tomorrow afternoon."

"Twila, do you refer to me as Auntie when you take those business calls?"

Twila scowled and grinned at the same time. "Maybe. Through habit. Why?"

"It makes me sound old."

"Old? Twenty-six? Don't be silly. Hell, you *are* my auntie. Like it or not."

"Nevertheless, the cuteness of being your auntie is wearing thin." Remembering Dave Andrews's response—assuming her niece would be a child—Renie winced and twirled spaghetti on her spoon. She took a big bite. "What else did Bryan say?"

"You need to concentrate on the underwater somersaults and holding your breath. He said he believes in you."

Renie swallowed. She gazed at her niece, who was cutting the spaghetti on her plate into tiny bits with a knife and fork. "Did he say anything about Cherry Bernard?"

"Who?"

"The other woman they're considering for the film."

"No. No Cherry. No banana. No grape. Stop worrying! Bryan wouldn't have brought you here and outfitted you with the loan of the tail, unless you were first choice."

"I'm *his* first choice. Someone else wants this Cherry. She is a champion swimmer," Renie said weakly; she was weary, she realized.

"So? And you're not?"

"Was, you mean. I'll never be the swimmer I was before the accident, and I have to accept that."

"You're good enough to be a mermaid, that's what counts here."

"Good enough, yes. Strong enough? I'm not sure."

Twila poured herself a glass of red wine. "You'll make it, Auntie Ren."

"I'd better. Bankruptcy doesn't appeal to my finer senses."

Her niece laughed. "And if—I mean when—you do get this movie role, you'll be rich. And famous. You'll be more famous than Flipper!" She munched her salad, rearranging the tomato slices in her bowl. "And I'll be there at your side all the way, wallowing in the sunshine of your success and trying to get noticed by your admirers—your castoffs."

Renie smiled. "And will you be at my side if I don't get the job?"

"I'm here now, aren't I?"

"Now doesn't count. We're sitting on a yacht on the French Riviera. This isn't your normal poverty."

Twila sighed contentedly. Her short, light brown hair framed her pretty face. She was wearing a purple T-shirt with an octopus on the front, and several gold chains of varying sizes. "You're right. This brand of poverty was worth leaving Gary for."

"Twila, what tripe! It's been eight months since you left Gary, and you talked about leaving him for three years before that. It wasn't to come here with me."

"You're right." Twila stretched her arms wide and smiled. "It was a marriage made in hell. And besides, one can't fight destiny. I was born for the yachting life. I'm my true self when I'm bobbing on the azure sea. This was my calling! Except, of course, for my role as ship's cook. But that will change soon. Let's have nothing but positive thoughts here, Auntie. You admitted that the screen test was the hardest part, and you did fabulously. Bryan Milstrom loves you. Mastering this fishtail problem is just a matter of practice. You're going to be picked for the role. I know it and you know it. You're getting stronger every day."

Renie nodded, wishing she could be as confident as Twila. "If only my back didn't get so tired."

"It just takes time after a long recovery. They will give you a chance to rest during the filming. I watched a movie being shot once. They kept starting and stopping all the time."

"With underwater cameras it will be a little more complicated."

Twila sipped her wine. "Just get the flippin' role. Once you've got it, they'll have no choice but to let you rest if you need to. Just get it, that's all you have to worry about right now."

"That and being seen while I'm trying to practice. I had the strangest feeling someone was watching me earlier."

"That's impossible! Isn't it? Weren't you too far from the shore?"

"Yes. And the cove is secluded, private property. There are no dwellings along there. I'm sure I just imagined it because I feel so silly in that idiotic costume. It's hard enough trying to get accustomed to going topless."

"Everybody goes topless here."

"Nevertheless, it takes getting used to."

Twila began to giggle and was soon doubled over with laughter.

"What is so funny?"

"The thought of you being seen. If you were, the news would probably hit the world press! Nobody could tell that costume from the real thing, even up close. If you were seen, we'd sure hear about it. The *world* would hear about it—on both sides of the Atlantic." She held up her hand, gesturing headlines. "Mermaid Sighted on the Côte d'Azur. Men of Calypso Dispatched to Area. Sea World Scientists Dispatched to Area. Greenpeace Ships Dispatched to Area. Navy Frogmen—"

"Stop that!" Renie howled. "I wasn't seen! Okay? I was just imagining things."

Still smiling, Twila studied her across the narrow ship's table. "On the other hand, we both know you've always had incredible intuitive powers, Auntie Ren."

"No more so than anyone else."

"Ah, but you recognize yours, that's the difference. Instead of pushing down your intuitive feelings, you encourage them, recognize them, and then act on them. I've always envied your ability to do that. I hope this time your intuition is wrong. Bryan Milstrom would not be happy if word of this film project got out before he was ready."

"I'm careful. The cove is deserted this time of year. Even the Gypsies have disappeared." Renie got up and stretched, grimacing. "I'm going to put the hot-water bottle on my back for awhile."

"You haven't eaten much."

Stretching again, Renie twisted a few times and bent to do some toe touches. "I'll have some dessert later. First I want to lie down for a few minutes."

She stepped into the galley. The water on the stove was still hot. She poured it into her hot-water bottle, wrapped a thin towel around it, and carried it to one of the berths that lined the bulkhead saloon. Lying down, she slid the rubber flask under the small of her back and moaned.

"You sound like a parrot with a mouthful of peanut butter," Twila said from the table, where she was still eating. "You're pushing this strenuous swimming."

Renie gazed at the ceiling and felt the gentle rocking of the boat. Soothing, like a cradle. It felt good to be riding on the ocean. "I know I'm pushing a bit, but I don't have much time. I need practice in open sea. Waves are so heavy."

Twila poured herself another glass of wine and gulped it down. "Do you want a couple sips of wine, by chance? Or some aspirin?"

"Neither, thanks. I'll be okay in a few minutes. I'm lying here, building up my mental powers to challenge you to a game of gin rummy."

Twila raised her glass in a salute. "Ah, to these lovely nights of leisure!" She wrinkled her nose and squinted into the burgundy bubbles. "Menless nights though they may be, damn all. But hey! Here's to leisure, starlight nights of gin rummy. Here's to leisure, rocking days in the world's most coveted sunshine. And here's . . ." She raised her glass still higher. "Here's to sexy French hunks, wherever the hell they're hiding."

"Speak for yourself about the leisure . . . *and* about the sunshine," Renie mumbled, eyes closed. "And about French hunks, too, for that matter. . . ." While Twila toasted herself on deck, Renie's days were spent below, or at least under cover of shade—a wide brimmed hat or umbrella—to be sure her light skin remained as pale as possible, like that of an underwater creature.

Bryan Milstrom favored her for the role because he had been the one who'd "discovered" her. The well-known producer-director had first seen her five years ago at an intercollegiate swimming and diving competition. She had placed first in two events at that meet. As far back as then, Milstrom had been brainstorming this project. But the timing was wrong; a mermaid movie had already been done. His own concept, a much different one, was put on hold, but Bryan had remembered the pretty blond collegiate swimmer, and found her five years later, when the project was a "go."

He had told Renée Lloyd he needed a woman who was an expert swimmer, who could spend days and weeks of shooting in the water, and who looked like her—light skinned, blond, with pale eyes and facial features of a delicate, classic beauty.

Milstrom had no way of knowing that in the interim a water-skiing accident had injured her back and put an end to her swimming competitions forever.

The accident had cost Renie dearly. It had brought her career as a swim coach to a halt, and just trying to put her life back together had eaten up her savings. All she had ever known or loved was swimming. The thought of having to give it up and start over in something else had been a difficult one to try to adjust to, especially difficult because she'd had no idea what that field would be.

Bryan Milstrom's representative had found her through the university, and, as luck would have it, at the university pool, practicing the therapy exercises. She'd had the presence of mind not to explain what she was doing, not to mention her injuries at all. By the time she left, she had agreed to a screen test.

Renie hadn't taken any of it seriously at first. Although she'd had three drama classes, the thought of a career in films had never occurred to her. It didn't particularly appeal to her, even now. But in her current state, broke and without a career, she couldn't pass up a chance like this. And the work was in the water. This was why it didn't frighten her. She loved the water.

The big question was: had she regained enough strength in her back to keep up what promised to be a grueling swimming schedule with the cumbersome mermaid costume? Every one of these practice days helped.

Where Cherry Bernard had come from, Renie didn't know. She'd never heard the name around collegiate competition, so Bernard couldn't be *that* good. Cherry might be more beautiful, though, Renie thought. And she probably was a better actress.

Renie forced her mind to clear. There was no point worrying over things that hadn't come about yet. The decision was still days away. . . .

She dozed. By the time she woke, Twila had taken away the dishes and was sitting on the opposite berth, painting her toenails and mouthing sentences in French from a book that lay open on the floor. A tape cassette was playing articulated French sentences over and over. *Pour aller à la gare, s'il vous plaît? Parlez plus lentement, s'il vous plaît.*

Renie listened to Twila repeating the statements. "What are you saying?" she asked sleepily.

"Please direct me to the station . . . and speak slower doing it. *S'il vous plaît*," Twila answered.

"Great, if we ever find ourselves in need of a station." Renie turned her head toward the square, curtained porthole. The lights on shore twinkled, and the night was black enough to hide the outline of the distant mountains. Above, in a cloudless sky, stars were shining brightly. The lights of the hillside village looked like stars, dropped into a sparkling bouquet. There were a hundred colors in the sparks of light.

She thought of Dave Andrews and wondered why he had chosen the little village of Cauvier as his home. It was an isolated place, one of many small villages along the Riviera. He didn't seem the type of man to repair engines for a living, but then he hadn't said he did it for a living. He hadn't said what he did, or where he was from in England. Well, there were expatriate Brits everywhere; it wasn't unusual.

His looks *were* unusual, she thought with a smile, unusually pleasing. One did not meet a man that handsome every day. A perfect body. Thick, dark hair. Beautiful, if mysterious eyes. He had looked at her as no man ever had—intensely, distractedly, as though he wanted to know her and at the same time distance himself from her. The man intrigued her.

Twila looked up from her French book. "What are you lying there thinking about, Auntie Ren?"

"I was wondering about the people who live in the village above the cove. They can look out from their windows and see the lights of the boats on the water. Our boat lights must look just like stars that have dropped down into the water. I wonder if the people on the hill ponder who we are, we who are floating out here, and I wonder what people in little hillside villages are thinking about on a warm September night like this." She said people. She meant Dave Andrews.

She turned to look at her companion. "You know, Twila, even if we were there—in the village—right now, we couldn't even talk to most of them."

Twila stretched out one leg and examined her toenail polish. "Speak for yourself. I'm on side two of my *Practical French* tape. I can order thumbtacks and I can ask for the pharmacy, the fish store and the veterinarian. And the station."

"You can ask, but you'll need luck being understood. You have the most unique French accent I've ever heard." Renie sat up slowly. Her back no longer ached. "Not that I've heard that many."

Twila turned off the tape and continued to mutter French phrases. She looked up from the textbook. "Do you remember when we were kids and we saw that old Esther Wilson movie on TV, and you—"

"Williams," Renie corrected.

"Wilson, Williams, whatever. You said someday you were going to be a movie star in a spangled swim costume, just like her. Do you remember?"

"Of course I do. I fantasized about it for years. That was the summer I started competing in the swim meets at Billings Park."

Twila smiled. "I was thinking about that today. I remember you sitting in your beanbag chair, telling me you were going to become a movie star. And now look what's happening! Maybe you were supposed to experience that horrible accident so that your real calling could come about!"

"Interesting theory," Renie said.

"And absolutely true. I've checked it out. Childhood fantasies are direct predictions of what our lives will be. It's a proven fact."

Renie grinned and rose to get a bottle of mineral water from the kitchen. Pouring, she asked, "What did you fantasize about when you were a kid, Twila?"

"Me? Why, yachts and villas and long, long limos with young, suntanned drivers. And gowns that caused gasps."

"Really?" Renie turned from the galley counter and sat down at the little table.

"Oh, yes. And handsome lovers. You see how different we are? You with your swimming dream that went up in smoke with one accident, and me with Gary? Well, life goes on." She set the book aside. "There have *got* to be some gorgeous male specimens on the French Riviera. I've always dreamed about alluring Frenchmen, but I haven't seen anything very handsome at the beach."

"I did, at the marina," Renie volunteered. "Not a Frenchman, but certainly handsome."

"You devil! Not French? What is he?"

"English."

Twila leaned forward. "Really? And?"

"And he's taking me to lunch tomorrow."

Sitting down at the table again, Renie sipped the mineral water, thinking about the *vin blanc cassis* Dave had bought for her. A little wine wouldn't hurt her; she was just so used to being "in training." Endurance training. This was like her old Olympic training, but oh, so different. If this role didn't come through, she wouldn't even have enough money to get home. . . .

Twila's cheerful voice cut through the gloom of her thoughts. "Did you tell the handsome Englishman that you're about to be a film star, Auntie Ren?"

"Of course not. You know I can't do that."

Walking on her heels because her toenail polish was still wet, Twila hobbled to the shelf, found a deck of cards and tottered to the table.

Renie took the cards from her and began shuffling.

Twila poured herself a third glass of wine. "So you are a woman of mystery to him. Someday your Prince Charming will see your face on the screen in front of him and know he is in love."

Renie laughed. "What Prince Charming is that?"

"The one in all our old games. Remember? He was always so mysterious, your prince. He came from a faraway kingdom, so far away you didn't even know where it was."

Renie smiled. "Oh, yes. The prince was exiled from his kingdom and could never go back. . . ." The kingdom, she remembered with amusement, was always England. England was the name of a faraway place that had a real queen and real princes. . . .

"Take note," her niece prophesied. "He will see you as a beautiful mermaid on the screen and he'll fall under your spell, and then he'll never rest until he finds you. It's how dreams work." She paused. "You're bending the hell out of those cards, Auntie Ren! Are you going to deal or not?"

How strange, Renie thought, *that Twila would be talking like this tonight.* And she remembered the feeling of being watched when she was lying on the rocky islet in the cove. There couldn't have been anyone near her.

Yet the feeling had been so strong.

4

RENIE STOOD under a clump of lotus trees near the marina entrance, waiting for him and feeling overdressed in the ankle-length skirt, white satin blouse and wide-brimmed hat, clothes for maximum protection from the sun. The day was bright and pleasantly warm.

A small French car pulled up to the curb and Dave Andrews got out, smiling, to open the door for her. He wore khaki trousers and a white shirt that set off his tan. The moment she saw him, she remembered exactly why she had so eagerly accepted his invitation.

"I hope I'm not late," he said. "Morgan and I had to have a discussion about his wanting to come."

"Obviously he yielded to authority."

"To bribery. He's home having a lamb chop." Dave closed the door and got into the driver's side. "I wish you wouldn't look at me like that, Renie. The people who had him first spoiled him rotten. I merely inherited the ghastly results. I've had no prior experience with his brand of insolence."

"But he is home and not here," she said with a smile. "Which is the main thing. Although I wouldn't have minded his company."

"You don't know what you're saying. He would be in the back, drooling down your neck." Dave turned onto the main road. "You look beautiful. Even more so than I remembered. I couldn't stop thinking about you last night."

Renie rolled down the window so the breeze could blow into her face. "What couldn't you stop thinking?"

"Just . . . about you . . . and about where you come from."

"You must meet many Americans vacationing here on the coast."

"Not . . . not really."

He seemed nervous, Renie noted, a little uncertain what to say every time he opened his mouth. He also kept glancing down at her legs. It wasn't a lecherous look, exactly; there was something sensually curious in it. Except for an unmistakable air of mischief, he did seem slightly unsure of himself . . . or of something. Probably he just couldn't understand why she was dressed like his grandmother.

"It must be fine living on the French Riviera," she mused, looking at the sky-blue sea shimmering in the sunlight and at the craggy shoreline ahead.

"Better in winter when the crowds are gone," he answered. He turned, glancing again at her legs. "Tell me about yourself."

"Oh, boring stuff. You first."

Dave frowned thoughtfully. "I'm a vagabond. I work when I have to and play when I can. Sun and sea. I enjoy boating and scuba diving. That's it. My life. You say you like the ocean." He had thought it over and decided he would talk about the other world—her ocean world—as casually as he could. It was the only way to gain some access to her secret, to open some channel to discover what she was and why she was here with him. "Ever tried scuba diving?"

"A few times, but I'm claustrophobic. I find all that equipment awfully confining. I like the feeling of freedom in the water," she said.

"Yes. There would be little point in your..." He ended his sentence with a smile. His eyes were fixed on traffic as the road began to twist.

"Little point in my what?"

He seemed not to have heard the question. "Sometimes," Dave said, "I've imagined how good it would feel to be a fish . . . to swim freely in the sea."

"How could anyone want to be a fish? Fish are such stupid creatures."

He was silent.

"A sea mammal, maybe. A dolphin or a cousin orca."

Cousin! his mind screamed. *A killer whale?* "Whose cousin?"

"The dolphin's cousin," she answered, looking at him very strangely.

"Oh," he said. "Yes."

"We might be dolphins," she mused. "At least they have interesting lives."

"They do? Swimming about the sea all day long? Is it interesting, swimming about the sea all day?"

She sensed he was goading her about something, but there was such a curious gentleness in his voice that she wasn't sure. She answered, "I only know that a species cannot develop such a complex brain without using it— without complex matters to think about. So, therefore, interesting things are going on in the sea."

"Mmm. I see I'm in the company of an expert on ocean life."

She shook her head. "Not an expert, just a fascinated observer. Goes along with my interest in swimming, I suppose. I took some marine biology classes in college."

"What college would that be?"

"The University of California at San Diego."

He was intent on probing for information, Renie thought. Maybe Englishmen were curious by nature. She, too, was curious. A man who lived in a country not his own . . . a man who looked too handsome to be wandering free . . . who claimed to be a vagabond but did not really look the part, except maybe for his deep tan. He had also been on the coast long enough to have mastered the French language.

"And you?" she asked. "An alma mater in England, perhaps?"

"Oxford. My focused interest in those long-ago days was business, if you can believe it."

"Not now?"

"Now I'm not the type. I discovered Africa. And I discovered the southern coasts and the sun."

Renie studied him. "What did you do after college, then?"

"A partner and I started a retail business in London."

"What sort of business?"

He glanced at her before he answered. "African art."

"You were the buyer, of course. Traveling Africa?"

"Yes. The business had problems, though, and I decided to leave it."

"When adventure called too loudly," she translated. "When the warm sea called, you had to go. Oh, how well I know that call...the lure of the warm coasts. Will you ever go back to England?"

"No."

She knows I cannot return to England, he realized. *I don't know how she knows, but she does. She knows the ocean can capture a man's love as surely as a woman can. She knows she, too, can capture me. Hell, she knows she already has.*

"I admire the vagabond life-style," Renie was saying. "Someday I'll be a vagabond, too."

She took off her hat because its soft brim was blowing too much in the wind, and leaned against the seat, feeling the warmth of the sun through the glass and the refreshing cooling of the wind. She began to hum, then to sing softly, a melancholy tune Twila had been playing over and over on the tape machine after the torture of the French lessons was over.

Dave fell into a silence that grew oppressive as the minutes passed. Renie turned her head just enough to see his hands gripping the steering wheel very hard.

"What's the matter?" she asked. "Is my singing that bad?"

"What?"

"You've gone tense as a pond frog since I started to sing, as if you can't stand it."

If you heard her singing, you would be doomed, Jean-Claude had reminded him. "Your voice is lovely," he said weakly. "It has a . . . it has a haunting quality."

"Does that disturb you?"

"I . . . it's the traffic. French drivers."

She scowled. "I hate to point this out to you, Mr. Andrews, but you drive exactly like the rest of them."

"A matter of survival."

"It's terrifying."

"I'm sorry. I don't want to terrify you."

"Well I . . . I trust you. Do you prefer I not hum that song, then?"

"No, of course I don't prefer it," he answered, but he didn't sound absolutely sure, and jumped quickly, almost desperately, to a different subject. "What do you mean, tense as a pond frog? Who ever heard of a tense pond frog?"

She laughed. "Frogs are extremely tense individuals. They sit in the reeds thinking of flies, or whatever it is frogs think about, and the least small footstep will send them leaping for the water. Did you ever walk along a quiet shore and listen to the plops and splashes?"

"You're taking me back to the carefree days of my youth." He slowed the car and turned into a widened area of the road that overlooked the sea.

They had been climbing steadily. To their left rose the rust-colored hillsides dotted with pines and scrub. On their right was the winding seacoast heavily built-up with hotels and yacht harbors. He pointed out landmarks, but Renie found it hard to concentrate on what he was saying. The subtle scent of his cologne reached her. His soft English accent rose and fell like music. She studied his hands as he talked. Well-shaped, masculine hands. His nails were not manicured but were nonetheless immaculately clean, in spite of the fact that he worked on motors. He must have cut himself on one; he wore a small bandage on his palm.

Vagabond, she thought. A carefree life. He had willed it so, but there was something not free about him. A certain look in his eyes, an inflection in his voice when he spoke of his life. She tried, but could not define it. *He is not a vagabond. Why does he say he is?*

The restaurant sat isolated on a small inland road, the sort of place that depended on verbal recommendations for its patronage. So popular in high season, it served only a few locals now in autumn when the tourists had gone back north.

They entered a terraced garden under an umbrella of trees. A fountain splashed into a lily-lined pond where goldfish swam. Flowers bloomed in old clay pots placed all around the garden and along the broken stone walls.

"It's wonderful!" Renie said, leaving Dave's side to respond to the draw of the splashing water. "A fountain sings nature's prettiest songs!"

Her heel sank into a recess on the rough flagstones and she lost her balance. Only Dave's quick reflexes prevented her from falling.

The warmth and strength of his arms as he caught her threw Renie more off balance than the broken stone had done. It was like hitting a warm sea tide and being caught in a current too powerful to escape. Powerful, yet so protective that sensations throbbed at his touch . . . sensations of having been in his arms before, sometime far out of memory.

When she was steady again—standing on her own, at least—he did not release her at once. Was it proof that he had been waiting for a chance to touch her, she wondered, or had he felt something, too? Either way, she knew for certain that he was attracted to her in the same way she was becoming attracted to him. The most dangerous kind of attraction.

Holding her against his body those few seconds had been a most deliberate way of making her aware of the danger of his touch. Yet somehow it had seemed less calculated than reflexive, like a first caress on velvet, when, try as one may, one cannot let go until the senses are satisfied.

"Are you all right?" Dave gazed at her curiously.

"Yes, thanks. I'm such a klutz. I'm not used to these shoes."

Again he looked at her legs. "The stones are warm. If you're not used to shoes, there's no reason not to take them off."

"I didn't say I wasn't used to shoes. I said I wasn't used to *these* shoes." Supporting herself with his arm, she pulled off the narrow-heeled shoes and padded toward the low wall of the pond at the foot of the fountain. Under the protection of the shade trees, she sat down, took off her hat and shook loose her hair. "I love gardens like this. Gardens are a compromise between civilization and nature, aren't they? I think the concept of harmony must have begun in a garden."

"Strange," he said pensively. "My mother used to say that very thing . . . with the same sense of awe in her voice that I hear in yours."

She gazed into the water. Sunlight glinted on the scales of the goldfish that swam lazily among the reeds. The song of the falling water, the warbling of birds and the chirping of insects mesmerized her. She felt the afternoon warmth on her shoulders. Gradually she became aware of Dave's eyes on her.

She looked up and caught him staring. His eyes were misted with a layer of something like disbelief. One gazed at a flaming sunset like that, but not another human being. Renie flushed with embarrassment.

To her surprise, he did not seem to notice. His gaze moved again to her legs and her feet.

"Dave?"

He took a step nearer and sat down beside her; the dreamy look remained in his eyes. Reaching out, he said in a monotone, "I think you have seaweed in your hair. . . ."

This remark startled her. "Seaweed? Oh, sure, I always go around with seaweed on my head. What's with you? I passed under the mimosa trees. I haven't dived into the pond."

"I was joking," he said, picking the tiny leaves from her hair.

"Your English humor eludes me."

His thigh was touching hers—very deliberately. That dangerous touch again . . . dangerous because its sensations moved along her thigh to her groin like rays of heat and caused the fluttering, that helpless fluttering. . . . She did not want to move away.

Who is this man? Renie asked herself. This man who made her so conscious of being a woman? Who looked at her as though she were not quite real?

THE SCENT OF FLOWERS perfumed the air. Reflections from the fountain silvered the overhead awning with dancing light. Gazing at him in the filtered light while they sat at the table in the garden, Renie ached to question him about himself, but didn't dare take it too far.

It would be inviting questions back, and she was not prepared to explain what she herself was doing in France.

I could love this man, she kept thinking. *I think I love him already, but how could I?*

He was doing something to make her want him! She feared he knew more about her heart than she knew herself. It was scary. Had she no control over falling in love with a vagabond stranger, who was indeed a stranger but only a fake vagabond? What the devil was really going on?

She ached to know who he was. Over her *crevettes*—a shrimp salad—Renie probed, "Were you ever married?"

He hesitated before he answered. "Yes." Technically he was still married, and he hated to be reminded. For the sake of conversation he asked, "Were you?"

"No. Do you have children?"

"No."

"Divorced?"

He nodded with visible discomfort. She thought, *He doesn't like the subject.* Whatever happened to his marriage, he wasn't over the pain. He was uncomfortable with all of her personal questions. Well, they were a good pair.

Dave did not act hungry. He avoided her eyes sometimes, probed her eyes at other times, ordered more drinks and kept drinking steadily. "If Morgan had not chased the cat onto the pier," he said, "I wouldn't have met you. Or would I? I have the feeling we were destined to meet and had no choice in the matter. And if it hadn't been the pier it would have been another place. What *is* destiny, Renie? Can you explain destiny to me?"

She set down her fork. "Can anyone explain it? I wonder if destiny is whatever we choose it to be. We *think* destiny isn't a choice, but actually, somehow, it is."

"Choice? Whose choice?" *Not his. Between a mortal and a mermaid, what free will has the mortal?* He was a victim—a helpless, handpicked, enraptured, cornered victim. "You're saying we chose yesterday, then, that moment on the pier? Who chose? Both of us or just one of us?"

Her eyebrows rose. Gentle laughter sparkled in her pale eyes. "If only one of us chose the moment on the pier, then which one?"

"You," he answered.

"Me? You think I chose to alter your destiny? How could I?"

"I hoped you'd tell me. By being there...being here...my life is changed. I don't know how...or why. Tell me why."

She laughed aloud and shook her head. "What is happening here, Dave Andrews? What are we talking about?"

"About the fact that we didn't meet by chance, and therefore I can't walk away from you. It would do no good for me to pretend you don't already have a hold on me."

Is it lust? he asked himself for the hundredth time. *Is that why she came?* To make him want her more than he had ever wanted a woman in his life?

To make him fall in love with her?

Neptune's magic or not, Dave hated himself for not fighting it. He didn't want to fight the erotic euphoria, already knew he wouldn't even try.

Renie said, "Destiny is an interwoven thing. I mean, if I had seen you before I met you, I'd have wanted to meet you. I admit it. There are people we're just ... drawn to."

He sipped his drink and looked at her suspiciously. "How much time do we have?"

She blinked. "You mean today?"

"No, I mean your time here ... on the coast."

"Oh. A few weeks." He was looking at her in that unnerving way again ... as if he were looking at a sunrise too magnificent to be real. As if she were an object of his unrestrained love. As if he couldn't help it.

He reached across the table and touched her bracelet of pearls, running his fingers sensually over each sea gem as if each was a part of her, each a reflection of an emotion unexplored, for him to seek and find.

His fingers trembled, causing the pearls to tremble on her wrist, making the light reflect shades of blue like those of the sea, like those of her eyes ... and his own.

His hand moved over hers. His heart beat faster when he touched her, and it would do no good for him to pretend otherwise, for she knew. She knew. Her eyes were the eyes of a woman who wanted him ... who wanted to possess his body and his soul. He had no will to fight her; to the contrary, he welcomed the challenge.

Whatever else she was at night, she was a woman now, in daylight, with the soft flesh and inviting lips of a woman whose beauty surpassed any other he had ever known. Whose musical voice enchanted; whose eyes dared. He welcomed the danger she presented.

After all, they were together in his world, and in his world she was flesh and blood.

"Tonight," he said softly, concealing his burning impatience to touch her again, "you cannot be with me because you have to be somewhere else." It was a statement, not a question.

She shook her head hesitantly, wondering what he was thinking. That she had another date?

"Nor tomorrow? Not ever nights, Renie?"

"Ever is too long. I'm tied up for a few nights."

"Like Cinderella . . . you disappear."

He smiled across the table. The overhead branches moved softly on his face. The splashing of the fountain filled the poignant silence. He was still holding her hand. "If I've had moments of stammering today, it's because I don't do particularly well at adjusting to a state of enchantment."

She squeezed his hand with affection. "How eloquently you speak."

"Eloquence has nothing to do with it."

"There, an example. It does. Take it from a girl who is accustomed to hearing, I dig you, babe."

He grimaced.

She laughed. "I dig you, Mr. Andrews."

He smiled oddly. "When you look at the stars over the sea tonight, think of me. Think of us together."

His words, spoken so huskily caused the fluttering in her loins to start again. It was as though the "us together" was a foregone conclusion, yet he wouldn't say it that way . . . except with his eyes. She imagined heat from every star in the night sky, like little heat points pricking her body . . . every star in the night sky searing, penetrating her resistance to him. His voice. His sensuous, challenging eyes. His breathing, moving rhythmically beneath the folds of his white shirt. His nearness made the dancing stars grow hot. And it was still many hours until darkness!

Oh, God—he knew.

He knew that every star of the night sky was on fire. Somehow he knew she would be watching the stars because he had asked her to.

"I'll be watching," Dave said, momentarily off guard.

She swallowed and tried to calm her pounding heart. "Watching?"

"The stars tonight, reflecting on the sea." *And you,* he thought. *I'll be watching you . . . on the mossy rock.*

He looked at his watch. The afternoon was nearly gone. She would be in the sea at twilight. "We'll have lunch again tomorrow, Renie."

As they left the garden, she felt as if she were floating. The buoyancy of new love had left her giddy. Anything was possible when there was love; she had known it when she saw the bright, multihued sun dog in the western sky. An omen of something beautiful to come. Even then she'd known this man would love her.

But for how long? His odd comments meant he was trying to tell her something . . . something he assumed she understood.

BACK AT THE MARINA, Renie was barely out of the car when she heard Twila's shrill call.

"Auntie Ren!" She hurried up to them. "I expected you back here half an hour ago. Didn't want to leave you stranded without a boat ride." She was looking not at her aunt, but Dave.

"I would have taken the harbor taxi," Renie answered, knowing Twila's concern about the boat ride was no more than an excuse to satisfy her curiosity.

"Not easily," she replied. "The boat is out of service today." Twila, wearing shorts and a thin white T-shirt with a flowered bikini top showing through, leered at Dave so brazenly that Renie became embarrassed.

Quickly she introduced them.

"You're English!" Twila exclaimed the moment she heard his voice. "Are you vacationing?"

"No, I live here," he answered.

"How exotic! How free of cold English fog!"

"Precisely."

As he looked from one woman to the other, it was obvious to Renie he was comparing the contrast in their appearances. Twila, with a towel and a rolled beach mat in her oversize bag, looked the part of a girl who partied steadily and hard. Her rich brown hair was flying loose, and over her shoulder hung a child's inflatable swim aid, a oblong green tube with a crocodile's head. The long-snouted crocodile had green eyes, yellow nostrils and a hideous, cruel grin. And Twila had been drinking. Dave must be wondering how the two of them could be related.

"Were there no slips available in the marina?" he was asking.

"We prefer to anchor out," Renie answered. "It's so peaceful on the open sea."

"Especially at night," Twila added. "Looking at all the lights from shore. The two of us are not about to try to park the boat in that narrow slip. We'd leave a wake of sternless hulls down every row. So it is a condition of our lease that we not navigate the harbor channels. Our landlord doesn't trust us."

Renie had noticed a change of expression on Dave's face when Twila mentioned their nights on board. *He's wondering what I do in the evenings. He thinks I'm with another man.* Hell, what else could he think? She had implied, after all, that she was vacationing, not working, yet her evenings were never free.

Dave offered, "If you should need help with the boat at any time, just let me know."

"If we sent a message in French . . . I mean, provided we could, would you understand it?" Twila wanted to know.

He grinned. "A wave of a handkerchief would suffice."

"Dave speaks fluent French, if that's what you're getting at," Renie said.

Twila looked him up and down again, even more approvingly. "Auntie Ren," she said slowly, as if she had a mouth full of ice cream. "Why are you always the lucky one? You come to France and find a hunk who can drive boats and even communicate in the local tongue. Now me, Dave, I've been looking for an authentic native. In France do you think I can find a Frenchman? I've been killing myself learning French. I bought two new bikinis. . . ." She adjusted the strap of her brightly striped beach bag. The huge, grinning crocodile bounced against her shoulder. "You must know dozens of Frenchmen, Dave. Why don't you introduce me to one?"

"Twila, I can't believe you just said that." Renie winced.

"Well, what's wrong with honesty? Here I am, a stranger in paradise, and no one to show me the true language of France. What do you say, Dave?"

"I'm trying to think if I—"

"We could make it a foursome, couldn't we? Go out on the town . . . go sailing . . . lie on the beach. . . ." She glanced at Renie. "Whoops, not the beach. Auntie Ren can't lie in the sun."

"Are you allergic to sun?" he asked.

"Oh . . . uh . . . no. It's just—"

"Just that the sun is so drying," Twila chimed in. "Terrible effect . . . it makes Renie's skin so scaly, and who the hell wants scales?" She burst into laughter.

Renie noticed Dave cringe. Before she could try to save her own dignity, Twila was at it again.

"Sans beach, then. You wouldn't want to end up with scales. But we could . . . four of us could do other things. What about it? Surely you know a charming Frenchman?"

"Cauvier is such a small village," he hedged, looking doubtful. "There is one lad, a friend who is down for a holiday, staying here in Savenay. I can't think of anybody else who might be worthy of you."

"Fine. One is enough." Twila's face suddenly darkened. "Does he speak English?"

"Yes."

"All right." Twila nudged Renie. "Do you hear that, Auntie? The horizon shimmers with promise."

Dave scratched his chin doubtfully. "You don't look too pleased about this idea, Renie. I assure you, my friend is an honorable man."

"Good Lord, I'm not Twila's guardian. I just hate to see you put on the spot. Blind dates can be disastrous. And I don't want to dampen the fun because of things I can't do.... I mean the sun ... and evenings...."

Twila leaped in. "Damn, Auntie Ren! You haven't *told* him?"

A deadly silence descended. Renie shot her niece a threatening glance. This was not the time to risk having Bryan Milstrom find out she was a person who wouldn't honor his request to keep quiet about the film.

"Tell me what?" Dave's voice was husky, his tone suspicious. Challenging.

Twila heeded Renie's warning, but in her own mischievous way. "Oh, I'm babble-happy," she said with a grin. "I've had two beers. Maybe three. Or more. I don't remember. It's nothing, honestly. And if you believe that, I'll sell you the state of Indiana." She leaned closer. "I'll only tell you this. Renie is not your average person. She has a very special secret. You would *marvel* if you knew!"

He squinted. "Would I?"

Renie was so used to Twila's impossible sense of fun, she could only smile. "My niece is trying to impress you to make sure you won't back out of this blind-date agreement."

Twila's words seemed to have a strange effect on him; Dave stared at Renie. "Yours is a captivating secret."

She flinched. He had said it as if he already knew. He couldn't, though. Bryan had not said a word to anyone when he was here; he'd been obsessive about it. No one knew!

Dave's eyes moved to her legs. Again. Almost reluctantly. He sighed so deeply his shoulders rose and fell, and a strange sadness filled his eyes. Renie could only interpret the sadness as having to do with some tortured emotions of his own.

"I'll see if I can find my friend tonight," he said softly.

"Great! He is passably cute, isn't he?" Twila asked, brushing her hair from her eyes. "I mean, from what I've seen of the locals, nine-tenths of them are below the waterline. But then there is that *tenth* Frenchman—" her lips formed a thoughtful pucker "—who stands so far out of the water even his toes aren't wet! Hell or paradise. There is no in-between here. That's my studied observation."

Dave shook his head in amusement. "I can't promise paradise."

Renie said, "Stop putting Dave in a vise. Why not just drop it? You can cast your own net, Twila. You're good enough at it."

"It's all right," Dave said. "I'll look into the matter." He turned to Twila. "After all, what is a holiday without learning a local dance?"

Renie took a step back and looked at her watch. "I've got to go."

"Tomorrow, same place?" he asked.

She smiled and nodded, and held her hat against a small breeze that was blowing from the sea. Dave kissed her cheek, then touched his lips lightly to hers as if to seal a secret they shared. He winked at Twila and got into his car.

Renie stared after him, still feeling the tingling warmth of his kiss. They *did* share a secret ... a sparkling and transparent secret. Today in a sequestered, dream-glazed garden they had found themselves bewildered and in love.

Evening was descending and with it the pleasant cool of night. They walked through the marina entrance and along the pier toward the catwalk where a motorboat was tied up near the far pilings. Their footsteps echoed. The harbor was unusually quiet.

"I can't believe you asked him to do that," Renie said.

"What's wrong? The guy was all for it."

"He didn't have much choice."

Twila grinned. "Of course not. He wants to keep seeing you. Notice how I played that? Dangling the catnip—you—in front of him. I saw how he looked at you." She looked skyward. "Hey, did you see it, too? You up there? Keep an eye on this lady—the guy wants her!"

Renie frowned and laughed simultaneously. *It's too late to escape those sensuous eyes,* she thought. *He has overpowered me already—as he meant to do.*

"He's gorgeous!" Twila said. As they stepped from the low catwalk into the small boat, the menacing crocodile's snout hit Renie in the head.

"What is that stupid crocodile thing?"

"My sea wings. You know I can't swim. It was my treasure find of the day. I've been bobbing over the waves in high style in this ferocious crocodile."

Twila was trying to balance all her gear in the boat. "I repeat, Dave is honestly and truly gorgeous, Auntie Ren. Who is he, anyway?"

"I don't know," Renie answered. "I haven't the faintest idea who Dave Andrews is."

"What does that mean?"

"He's like a mysterious force, tangling up my life. He is pure male perfection, Twila. So innocently seductive, but anything but innocent. And he is concealing something about himself."

"Oh, intrigue! Wow! Not to worry, Auntie Ren! Leave this matter to Twila. I'll find out who he is."

5

DAVE DROVE UP THE HILL toward the village with his head spinning. *Renie Lloyd cannot be half fish, no matter what the hell I think I saw.*

But hard as he tried to talk himself out of it, Dave knew what he had seen. Twila, having consumed several beers in the sun, seemed to think Renie should have told him. How would she do that? Say, "Oh, by the way, Dave, would it be a problem for you if you knew I'm not a human being?"

Hell, yes! It was a problem!

He was already in love with her.

Wasn't it true that no man could have a mermaid? For very long? Wasn't it true that he loved her because she'd willed it through superhuman powers of some kind? Damn. Maybe he should try to run from her as he had run from everything else in his life. But he wouldn't . . . couldn't . . . didn't want to. . . .

His life was a new and vibrant fire with her in it, and he ached for the flames and the warmth and the incredible mystery of her.

AT HOME he fed a demanding Morgan his dinner and put in a call to Tristan Escoiffier, who had come down from Paris only a few days ago.

Tristan answered the phone chewing on something. He spoke in French. "Ah, Davey! Good you tele-phoned. I am bored with sailing. Why not meet me for a boules game and dinner?"

"Why not?" Dave answered. They were careful of their phone conversations because of the chance that Tristan's phone was bugged.

"The Grand' Place?"

"No, not Cauvier. Savenay. I'll call for you at eight." This was a coded way of telling Tristan that he wanted private time, to talk.

"Good. Until eight, then."

I must be out of my mind to do this, Dave thought when he hung up the phone.

He looked at his watch. It was nearing the time he had seen the mermaid on the rock the past three eve-nings. So it was back to the unnamed cove for the third time, because no power on earth could keep him away. He changed into jeans and sneakers, took his binocu-lars from the shelf, and locked Morgan in the garden.

HE KNEW she would be there. She was. He focused the binocular lenses on her face. No doubt remained, no doubt at all, that Renie and the mermaid were one and the same. During their lunch today he had looked for identifying marks—a tiny scar on her upper lip and a mole on her temple near her hairline. The binoculars were strong enough for him to see the mole.

Renie had a secret, all right!

How in the name of science and myth combined could she change from one form to the other? Did she have control over the change, or, like Cinderella, did she change at the stroke of a clock? The mental picture of the transformation was more than he could bear.

"Stop thinking!" he told himself. "Stop it!" He raked his fingers through his hair in frustration. Thinking made it a thousand times worse.

Tonight she did not stay long on the rocks, perhaps because there was some wind. When Dave watched her disappear into the waves, he was overtaken by a sadness so great it immobilized him.

The sadness would not let up. He made his way back up a slope where summer's wild lavender was still blooming in spots of shade in the dampness. He found himself thinking of her as a woman—a woman he wanted to know. This stupid agreement to introduce Renie's so-called niece to a friend was just a desperate ploy to try to find out more, any way he could, about who Renée Lloyd really was. And to buy himself some assurance that he would see her again before the day came when she would disappear into the sea forever. As mermaids always did.

Dave had vowed never to do this—never to let his guard down—and here he was, doing it consciously, calculatingly. And not because of a mermaid. Worse. Because of a woman.

The sadness lay in the knowledge that she was only an illusion.

While he had no other secrets from Tristan Escoiffier, he had to keep this one to himself. The impulse to introduce the two of them had been a stupid move. For the first time, he was allowing himself to do something risky.

The pain again. Dull now, but enough to block off the present and pull him back into memory...the ever-present reminder that he owed his life to that pain....

I see Tristan Escoiffier at the crowded market festival in Cauvier. Few men know what Escoiffier looks like, because very few photographs of him have ever been taken, but I have learned more about men who hunt terrorists than I ever wanted to know. Escoiffier is one of those men.

When Tristan turns up in the Cauvier marketplace on the second day, I approach him at a stand of black ceramic pots, and strike up a conversation in French, or try to. After only three months in France, my French is still shaky. Tristan helps me out; he speaks English fluently. We end up in the bar, where I eventually get around to inquiring whether the detective's services are for hire.

Laying out my dilemma before a stranger is an enormous risk. If anyone discovers I am alive, I will be one of the most wanted men in the world. Tristan might haul me in to Scotland Yard right here and now, and be applauded for it. But Escoiffier plays differently; I counted on that. Why bother with a renegade Englishman who is guilty only of screwing up his own life, when there is bigger quarry?

Only I can identify the terrorists responsible for blowing the plane out of the sky. Sitting in the corner of a dark French bar, we seal a gentleman's agreement with a drink: Tristan will not reveal his source until the terrorists are arrested. Only then will I venture out of exile.

We don't have time to waste. If any persons, including the terrorists, learn David Collister is alive, I will be arrested or killed within hours, depending on who finds me first.

Nearly two years have passed. Tristan's group has been able to identify the suspects, but they have yet to be caught. Each day comes with increased danger. Only three days ago, Tristan tried to talk me into surrendering to the law, but surrendering means jail. David Collister, alias Dave Andrews, will not surrender to the law . . . until I have to.

NOW, approaching Escoiffier's apartment, Dave knew that even though they had become friends, this "blind date," as Renie called it, was going to seem far out of line. He would not be able to explain it with any degree of logic, because there was no logic involved.

Tristan was waiting on the front steps of his building, smoking and reading a newspaper under the lights. When he saw the car, he rose and gave a short salute.

Dave pulled up and parked. "Anything of interest in the paper?"

"Nothing of interest to us."

Blond, hazel-eyed, Tristan Escoiffier was a man who seemed to have no age, a rare individual who could pass for a twenty-five-year-old or a forty-year-old with only a change of clothes and mannerisms. Dave knew he was actually thirty-six. Although he had never married, sometimes women resided with him at his Paris apartment. Dave knew he could not be classified "below the waterline" by Twila or anyone else. Shorter than Dave,

Escoiffier was a handsome man and very fond of women.

They walked toward the lights of the beach resort of Savenay, down a promenade lined with trees and quivering mimosas. The night was quiet. Lights from the marina on the north side of town cast a gauzy gold haze into the sky. A cool breeze blew from the sea.

Tristan, who always complained about the wind, was dressed in a dark blue sweater. He blew a great billow of smoke from his mouth.

"Why are you smoking?" Dave asked. "You don't smoke."

"I'm beginning to. I hear it is good for the nerves."

"You're as mad as a rabid dog."

Tristan laughed. "I do not want to grow old, *mon ami.* I could not stand being old." He puffed again, diligently and with concentration, like a student learning a skill. "What is on your mind, Davey?"

"A lady wants to meet you."

The Frenchman halted. "What? What lady?"

"It's not you specifically.... An American lass on holiday asked me if I could produce a Frenchman... for an escort. Poor girl, she insists it must be a Frenchman because of some foolish fantasy about Frenchmen being charming. I think it's a result of cinema propaganda."

"What would a cold-blooded Englishman know?" Tristan eyed him with grave suspicion. "What has brought this on? What have you been up to? Parties with holidaymakers? I did not think you were... What do the Americans say? A party duke!"

"I think you mean dude." He wasn't sure, though.

"Wrong. A dude is a cowboy. If you cannot speak American, how did you manage to communicate with this American girl?" Tristan kept looking at the cigarette in his hand. The American cowboy boots he was wearing with his tight jeans clicked softly on the walk. Turning to Dave, he changed his tone. His voice grew soft. "What is this really about?"

"Just what I said. I met a truly lovely lady who is here on holiday with her niece. I say niece, but that's misleading, because the two are the same age. The niece, Twila, asked me to introduce her to a Frenchman. That simple. She's quite a pretty lass. I think—"

"Are you out of your mind?"

"Not completely, no. I'm only talking about carrying on as men normally do, escorting young women about. I don't think typical male behavior is conspicuous. A boules game. A meal. A couple of women. What's the difference?"

The Frenchman raised both arms. "You are rationalizing. Dangerous. It is not good for you and me to be seen too much together, even in these small ways. And you know it." He paused, squinting. "Why would you want to?"

"Because I am interested in this woman I met. I have to find out more about her."

"Why?"

"Why? Because I am not a bloody monk! Why do you think?"

"I think it is temporary insanity. I hope it's temporary. You have no room in your life for—well, for women, perhaps—but for a *special* woman . . . no."

"What life are you referring to? I have no life. I'm getting sick of it, Tristan. You're supposed to be helping, but the years just go dragging on."

The other man touched his shoulder. "No need to become angry. I am not a man without an understanding heart. I think the end of our search is close. We must not put your safety in jeopardy now. And most certainly not the woman's."

As they neared the center of Savenay the promenade widened. Beds of flowers were planted in the center, and wooden benches stood along the path under the overhanging branches of the trees. Dave sat down on one of the white benches.

"All right. Suppose we just have a quiet lunch, the four of us. Twila wants to go to the beach, I think. Go to the beach with her, say a few phrases in French-tortured English. She only wants to have a bit of fun. The lady is quite extroverted and I think you'll like her. Who would think anything of it?"

Tristan sat down beside him and put out the cigarette with elaborate ceremony. "They could both be spies."

Dave growled. "Thank God I'm not in a profession like yours that makes a man mistrust everybody on the planet. You're dangerously paranoid."

Tristan laughed. "Perhaps, yes. But remember this, *mon ami,* as long as you yourself risk being identified, any woman whose company you keep could become involved in this nasty business."

Renie would probably not be in danger, Dave reminded himself. *Mermaids don't die; they can escape into their other world.* "It won't come to that," he said.

"The saints had better have some mercy for us both because you, my pathetic friend, are in love!"

Dave shook his head in meek denial. "Nothing will come of it, I swear."

The Frenchman looked at the clear night sky. Stars were twinkling and a half moon hung above the sea. "Ah, Davey! You know that billions of people in the world lead such mundane lives! Every day, every year they live almost the same from birth to death. They know little danger, they take no calculated risks. Would it not be hell?"

Billions of people, Dave thought. *And I'm the one who has to meet a mermaid.* He answered, "Sometimes I think a little normality might be a welcome thing."

Tristan laughed. "This, then, is how we differ most."

It was true. Escoiffier thrived best in dangerous situations. So why not play to that? "Are you afraid of meeting an American woman?"

"Afraid?" The hands rose again. "Only for my investigation. If you manage to get yourself killed before you identify my suspects, I lose my credibility. *I would not appreciate that.*"

"Spending a few hours with a woman when you're on holiday isn't going to get me killed and you know it. American women must scare you."

This brought a gusty laugh. "American women find me impossible to resist!"

"So prove it." Dave rose and began to walk again, hands in his pockets.

Tristan followed. "Very well. But I do not understand this."

"Certainly you do."

"No. There is something else you are not telling me. I will find out what it is."

Damn, Dave thought. *He probably will.*

But Dave knew he could no more resist Renie than the sailors of those ancient legends could resist the lure of mermaids, once those sailors had been targeted. For reasons only she knew, Renie had set her sights on him, lured him with every intention of seducing him, and he would not stop her. He couldn't if he tried, because he was bewitched. Tristan had called it love. Enchantment or love? Whichever it was, he was under its spell.

If this stupid scheme gave him even a few more hours with her, it was worth it. Any chance to learn more about her was worth the slight risk of more openly hobnobbing with Tristan Escoiffier, a man who always ran the risk of being watched by someone or other. They'd sometimes had their quiet boules games in the little village square on the hillside. They'd drunk in the bar on occasion. But always in Cauvier. Never here in Savenay on the coast. Never with strangers.

Until now.

"Just one thing," he said to the Frenchman as he watched him light up another cigarette. "Don't wear your cowboy boots tomorrow."

THAT NIGHT the Prince of Lost Clouds and his friend the Fir Bolg Soldier plotted a path through the Magic Land of Freedom to reach the Far shore, where Silka the Mermaid lived.

Dave wrote into the late hours, roughly sketching scenes with a pencil on a pad beside his computer. His sketches were used by skilled professional artists as guides for the illustrations. He had never met the illustrators of his books and never would.

The Wizard's Fireside Tales were more than a means of earning a living. They were journals, well disguised—perhaps not so well disguised—that chronicled his life. The lost clouds floated farther and farther away while the Wandering Prince fumbled his way from exile into limbo.

As Dave had done.

The Prince of Lost Clouds and the Fir Bolg Soldier had a mission. They had to reach the Far Shore in time to save Silka from the two fierce goblin villains, the three fingered Fireskog and the Hairy Grig.

Had Dave been able to draw with any skill, he might have put human faces on the goblins. And on the Fir Bolg, who was blond like Tristan. And, of course, on the mermaid.

He wondered what the Halfling Prince would do on the day Silka swam away and disappeared.

Perhaps it would serve the prince right. After all, he had left his elfin homeland to seek the silver rainbows . . . and never said goodbye. Now it hurt.

As Dave hurt.

Dave had never said goodbye. Not to his wife, not to anyone. He closed his eyes and thought of Sarah, and how her betrayal had chipped at his heart until he couldn't feel love anymore. He had not felt anything for so long. Maybe he would never feel love again. . . . Maybe it was not love surfacing from the ashes of his wife's betrayals now, but enchantment. The spell of a sorceress. . . .

I have translated my life into a fantasy, he thought. *And I'm paying the price for it now.*

He stared into the blank computer screen and thought of that last week in London, the week before David Collister had disappeared. Fights with his wife, not only about their business problems, but about her affair with the man who managed their auxiliary shop. David had left without confronting the other man, something he should have done to satisfy some primitive instinct within him, but the truth was, he hadn't cared. He hadn't been in love with Sarah for a long time. Nor she with him.

And he'd been ill. The pain from the stomach ulcer had been getting worse.

The pain had been severe for days, but on this morning of my flight to Africa, it has let up for several hours. Carrying the briefcase containing nearly £ 400,000, I tell Sarah it is to be my last buying trip. Either we maneuver the business out of the red with this next shipment of primitive art, or I will pull out. She has inherited controlling stock from her father. She and her lover can take over, implement their half-witted, unworkable ideas about making profits. I'm just about finished—with the import business and with my marriage.

It turns out that everything is finished already, but the morning I leave for Heathrow, I have no way of knowing it.

TWILA WORE a flowered cotton sundress and carried the beach bag and the inflatable crocodile. Renie was in pale blue silk and pearls. Dave parked in a No Parking area nearby. Tristan was late.

Just late enough to make an entrance, if one could call rushing down the promenade in shorts, a T-shirt and sandals an entrance.

He glanced quickly from one woman to the other and reached for Twila's hand, which he honored with a quick feather kiss. *He's good*, Dave thought. He had recognized Twila without a description. His insight was uncanny.

So was his charm. Twila was clearly delighted.

They drove two blocks to a small café on a side street for aperitifs and lunch. By the time lunch was over, Twila and Renie knew a great deal about Tristan's home, Paris, and Twila ached visibly to learn more. She and Tristan decided to go to the beach while the sun was still shining. Rain was forecast for the late afternoon.

Dave and Renie left them in the resort and drove to Cauvier, taking the small road that wound along the river past vineyards and green fields. The higher they climbed, the broader was the view of the coast.

Alone again, they could look into each other's eyes as they had not dared to do with Twila and Tristan watching their every move.

"What do you fancy?" he asked in a steady voice. "A drive up this scenic road to the mountains? A drink in the village square? Or can I offer you a drink on a quiet veranda of my own?"

As they drove, silky strands of Renie's golden hair flew loose from the ribbon meant to hold them in place at her neck, and in the sunlit breeze they blew about her face like wisps of gold glitter. Her mouth was small. Her full lips shone with a pearly-pink lipstick. Each time Dave saw her, he was more dazzled by her beauty.

"I'll choose your veranda," she answered brightly. "I'd like to see where you live."

The road skirted the village. They circled to the north and turned onto a narrow dirt road at the top, level with the steeple of the village church. Dave stopped alongside one of the front gardens that formed a keyboard along the row houses. His was the one at the end.

She gazed at the narrow, three-story house. "What a great view you must have!"

"The view was my reason for buying it."

Morgan, leaping at the gate, barked a greeting.

"Hello again, Morgan," Renie said; Dave opened the gate, repeating warning threats to his dog about jumping onto guests.

He led her through the narrow entry and into what she supposed was the living room, although it looked more like a study, with bookcases on all the walls, a desk covered with notebooks and papers and a computer. It did not look like a room for entertaining or relaxing.

"It looks like the house of a writer," she said. "You didn't tell me you were a writer."

"No one knows I am, except Tristan, who finds it an enormous joke. I write under a pseudonym. It's just easier because I like my solitude, and it adds an air of mystery to the books, which pleases the publisher. My mates at the local bar would tease me unmercifully if they knew about my books."

Her eyes scanned the desk for some clue. "Do I dare ask what you write, then?"

Dave smiled. "*The Wizard's Fireside Tales*. Fantasy stories for children."

Her mouth fell open. "You? Fantasy?"

He rubbed his chin. "I'm not particularly fond of them, Renie, but I have to make a living. They are gaining a following in Britain because kids like the characters—goblins and brownies and giants and fairies and a mermaid...the little people, we Brits call them."

"A mermaid? What a coincidence."

"Why?"

She met his eyes, then looked away. "Oh, I just adore mermaid stories. Let me see."

She did not wait for an answer, but went to a crowded bookshelf and picked up a copy of *The Wizard's Fireside Tales* by W.W. Wizard. She thumbed through the book. Its brightly colored drawings were beautiful, frightening, mystical, alive.

"It isn't my artwork," he said, watching her. "I only write the stories."

Fascinated, she carried the open book to her seat, reading. "The Prince of Lost Clouds? What a handsome prince."

"He's half elf, half human."

Renie smiled. "I see. And this hideous monster?"

"The three-fingered goblin called Fireskog. There with his evil sidekick, the Hairy Grig."

"How did Fireskog lose his fingers?"

"In a skirmish with a tribe of trolls. In the first book."

"Oh, it's a series. This is adorable, Dave! I'm just amazed. Where is the mermaid?"

"She appears for the first time in the story I'm writing at present. I haven't finished it yet."

Renie was thoughtful. "How interesting. Your mermaid, I mean."

"Why?" he asked again.

She cocked her head, looking coy. "Oh...I'll tell you sometime...perhaps sometime soon.... Oh, these terrible goblins! They'll give me nightmares." She couldn't put the book down.

"You'll tell me *what* sometime?" he prodded. If she could only say it, it would lift the veil that created the invisible barrier between them. But she would not. Because she was playing a game with him. A game of seduction at its finest.

"I'll tell you about the mermaid," Renie answered, "but not now. Dave, please let me borrow your books. You can swear me to secrecy, if you like, so your child side will be safe from your macho, teasing buddies. But let me read them."

"If you like," he said.

She scouted the shelf and found the remaining four in the series, hugging them to her chest as if she had found a treasure. "Do you believe in magic?"

"Of course. I always have."

"That's good." Renie smiled.

"Why is it good?"

"Because I believe in it, too."

On the far side of the room French doors led onto a terrace edged with trees and thick with ferns and flowers. He led her out there and motioned her to a wrought-iron table and chairs that stood in the shade. He dusted one of the chairs and bade her sit down.

Morgan settled himself strategically under the table with a contented sigh, his head resting on his front paws and a tennis ball in his mouth.

"I like your house," she said. "It's charming."

He had not yet sat down. "The poor old house was long neglected and needs major repairs. I'm gradually getting it done. When I've finished converting the loft into an office, then I can clean up my mess downstairs. What can I get you to drink?"

"Nothing at the moment. Your view is intoxicating enough." Renie rested her feet on another of the chairs and sighed.

He sat down beside her.

"So," she said. "I've learned something awfully interesting about you."

"Hmm. Now how about sharing your secret? The one Twila was talking about."

"Oh, yes, Twila and her runaway mouth. I can't tell you without breaking a trust, but I will tell you soon, honestly. I wish you wouldn't look at me like that. It's just to do with my career. Twila makes such a big deal out of everything."

He looked at her in amazement. "We most certainly wouldn't want to make a big deal out of it," he said sarcastically.

She wrinkled her nose. "Well, it's not as if I were married or engaged or something."

"Ah, well, in that case . . ."

She sat forward. "You're a fine one to talk, the way you speak so guardedly about your past."

"I have no past."

"That's what I mean."

Renie rose and walked to the edge of the garden; she stood at the low wall, looking over the red tile roofs of the village just below. A warm afternoon breeze whispered over the bright pink blossoms of the bougainvillea along the garden wall and scattered some of the petals over the ancient stones.

Her back to him, she said, "I love it here in this garden."

Dave got to his feet. The dog jumped up and followed at his heels, carrying the tennis ball. Dave moved alongside her and slid his arm around her waist. Constantly held captive in an uncomfortable state of wonder, he thought it a miracle just to touch her. To feel her softness and the warmth of her skin.

Renie responded by settling contentedly into the bend of his arm.

When she turned toward him, he gently touched her face, giving tiny feather strokes to her cheek, her chin, her lips, luxuriating in her beauty.

"How beautiful you are," he whispered.

"I find you very beautiful, too," she whispered back.

He could feel more than hear her catch her breath at his touch. Her lips parted as his fingers trembled across them. Her blue eyes, sparkling, gazed into his so deeply he felt she was looking into his soul.

What she saw there, he could not guess. Perhaps she had the power to read his mind, and if so, she knew that touching her was making him crazy with the most uncontrollable arousal he had ever experienced. Either his touch, his thoughts, or both caused Renie to tremble, too, and she moved closer to him. She looked into his eyes and her message was clear. She was anticipating his lips ... wanting them ... wanting ... asking. ...

His arm tightened around her and drew her gently closer. Softly he moved a strand of her blowing hair from her cheek and bent to kiss her.

The sensation sent him reeling. There was something so familiar in her kiss, as though he had kissed her a thousand times before in some mysterious, murky past ... or in some mist-filled dream. Yet simultaneously her kiss was new, primitive, and so fiery it turned his senses into flame.

Their lips drew slowly apart, but the gaze of their eyes did not separate. A hundred questions filled her sea-blue eyes. His eyes asked questions back.

Questions with answers—one answer. Words could not have said it better. The magic was dancing around them like burning stars.

I don't know or care who you are, her eyes were saying, *but I want you.... Whoever you are, I love you....*

He bent closer and kissed her again, deeply, open-mouthed and unrestrained, pulling her tightly against his body. She trembled again, allowing his primal emotions to tease and ignite her own.

The message in the passion of his kiss was as savagely intense as hers.

6

Dave's kiss stirred up as much fear as desire. She didn't want to want him. Not like this. Not as much as this. The timing was impossibly bad. She had neither the time nor the energy for a hot, intense romance with a free-spirited Englishman.

While Renie's head was telling her all this, her body quivered with the runaway emotions of needs long unfulfilled. She forced herself to pull away. Her breath came in little gasps.

He took both of her hands, and his hands were warm and large and strong. The magic hung about their heads like silvery mist. He cleared his throat. "Renie, this fierce attraction to you is unmanageable."

"The attraction is obviously mutual," she answered, keenly aware of the subtle scent of his aftershave. She had felt the hunger of his mouth, tasted the astounding power of his passion.

"Are you working magic on me?" he asked huskily.

She smiled. "I'm having enough trouble trying to deal with the magic you're working on me."

"I'm not doing it deliberately."

"Oh? And I am?"

"Aren't you, Renie?"

As she looked at him, very suddenly the sun shot from a bank of gathering clouds, releasing a stream of light so strong it momentarily distorted her vision. The brightness reflected by the whiteness of the wall directly hit Dave's eyes, turning their blue to silver. For a split second she was reminded of the face of the Prince of Lost Clouds on the jacket of his books.

And something more shone through the blinding light—that mysterious thing in him she had been unable to identify before—loneliness.

"Aren't you?" he repeated.

"What?"

"Bewitching me?"

Blinking in the sunlight, she answered very softly, as if to herself, "If I only could."

"You can," he whispered. "You have."

A man like Dave Andrews would be lonely only by choice. Why would he choose loneliness? What is the sadness in him? What does it mean?

"The timing is sort of bad," she said, hearing her voice shake.

"You didn't plan . . . the timing?"

"You're saying strange things again, Dave. What do you mean, did I plan it?"

He shook his head, bewildered. "The timing is bad for me, too, Renie. My life is rather a mess."

This remark was completely unexpected. "Is it? From my angle your life looks so uncomplicated, free of schedules and the everyday stress that most people complain of."

His smile was slow and wistful. The sun moved back behind the cloud bank, and his eyes darkened with the sky. "That's true," was all he said.

"And the quiet days," she continued. "And your house and your friend Morgan and the Wizard's wonderful tales. It all seems so lovely. What is a mess about your life?"

He didn't answer.

She felt the heaviness that seemed to drag his shoulders down. "Can't I pry?"

Still hesitation. "I'm trying to work out some problems with my past."

"You said you had no past."

He nodded knowingly, sadly. "As a matter of fact, I'm still working it out. I'm not as free as I appear. But you aren't, either, are you?"

"No...." she admitted. "My work could get awfully demanding."

"Your work...yes."

"Dave, what the hell are we talking about? Are we saying we don't have time for each other? Because if we are, then this is the most stupid conversation I have ever heard in my life."

He grew thoughtful. "We sound like two frightened people trying to warn each other away. Thinking we should. Not wanting to."

"Are we frightened? Is that it? Oh, it is, isn't it? What are we afraid of?"

"Of the intensity of the fire," he answered. He closed his eyes and held her close. "We're afraid of the intensity."

Renie, in his arms, allowed his strength to flow into her. Dave had incredible strength; she could always feel it around him...not just physically, but also emotionally. He was a man capable of withstanding almost anything. Even loneliness.

Finally she said, "I started this, didn't I, by saying the timing is not the greatest. I'm a little worried about my coming work schedule. But so what? And so what if your life was once a mess? What has that to do with now and the way you kissed me?"

He hugged her tightly, in silence.

She whispered, "I can handle the intensity if you can."

He cupped her face in his hands and gazed at her. In a moment he was kissing her, and the kiss shut out the clouds, the rustling of the wind and the fears, and there were only the two of them . . . a man and a woman . . . alone.

"It's so late," Renie whispered, her voice trembling once more. "I have to get back. . . ."

"I know. We'll go."

Renie felt intoxicated without having drunk a drop. She had waited a lifetime for a man who could make her feel like this. Dave Andrews had made it worth the wait.

SEVEN KILOMETERS down the hill, in Savenay, Tristan and Twila were waiting at the sidewalk café opposite the marina. Because the air was cooling with a thickening layer of clouds moving in overhead, Twila was wearing an oversize sweater.

"Where have you two been?" she asked over the sound of a passing car as they approached on foot.

"We thought you would be too occupied to miss us," Dave said.

Immediately Renie sensed something different. Not about the way Twila looked at her, but the way she looked at Dave. Her niece was staring at Dave with an expression of mixed contempt and awe. It frightened her. Had Tristan done something? Was she blaming Dave?

But it was clearly not Tristan. Twila turned and looked at him with open adoration. What, then? *What on earth could Tristan have been telling her about Dave? What did he know about him?*

"Is everything all right?" Renie asked.

"If you mean did we have a fine afternoon together, *oui*, we did," Tristan replied with an easy smile.

Although obviously preoccupied, Twila made an attempt at conversation. "Tristan is trying to teach me to swim without my crocodile," she said, and turned to the Frenchman at her side. "But he is such a wicked, adorable crocodile, and I love to float on him."

"Everyone stares at the crocodile," Tristan remarked good-naturedly. "Ah, but who cares? We had a supreme day, even when the clouds came in."

"What are those books you're carrying?" Twila asked.

"Oh, just . . . books I thought I'd like to look at."

"You mean you've been shopping for children's books? What does this behavior signify, dare I ask?"

"The books are written in English," Renie told her, as if that explained anything.

"As if you had time to read," Twila said. She sounded vaguely irritated.

Renie noticed Dave and Tristan exchange a glance; it happened so quickly, they could not have expected anyone to catch it. Was it about Twila? Or about something else?

"Where have you two been?" Twila asked.

"We drove up to my house above Cauvier," Dave answered.

Twila turned to Renie. "Is it a nice house?"

"Yes, very old and charming. I like it."

Looking at Dave with that odd expression, Twila said, "It must have cost a lot of jewels, huh, Dave?"

"Jewels?"

Tristan cleared his throat once, then again. Renie saw that he was trying to hold down laughter, but in the end he couldn't. His shoulders shook, and he began to chuckle.

"What is so bloody funny?" Dave demanded.

Tristan rose to his feet. "I must go." He reached for Twila's hand and kissed it lightly, with a smile. "I will call for you tonight, *mademoiselle*. For dinner at a quiet country inn." He looked at the others, his eyes dancing with amusement. "Will you two join us tonight?"

"I can't get away for dinner," Renie said.

Dave said nothing at all. He just stood there, looking from Twila to Tristan, wondering what the devil was going on.

RENIE DIDN'T GET A CHANCE to ask until they were aboard the *Sandrine II;* it was too difficult to talk over the motor of their harbor taxi.

The sky had gone dark with the threat of rain, so they hurried below and turned on the lights in the cabin.

"Okay. Let's have it!" Renie demanded before they sat down. "Why were you looking at Dave as if he were Jack the Ripper?"

Twila chuckled into the bunk room and called back, "I told you I'd find out about him, and I did! You're not going to believe who he really is!"

Moments later she emerged wearing sweats, carrying jogging shoes and socks.

"What on earth did Tristan tell you?"

"Not Tristan. A guy from Dave's village. We met him playing volleyball on the beach." She sat down and began pulling on her socks. "I had already asked Tristan a bunch of questions about Dave, and he said they were only casual friends who met talking in a bar and he knew nothing about his life."

"I didn't know you were going to snoop and spy," Renie said. "I don't—"

"Sure you did," Twila interrupted, pulling on a shoe. "I promised I would, didn't I? Oh, I know you don't pay attention to me when I say things, but I am not the fluff ball you take me for. I can spy with the best of them."

A surge of anxiety and anger rushed through Renie's veins. "Damn it! Will you just tell me what happened!"

"Okay! Okay! We had this great volleyball game, you know, and then we went for a cold drink and this guy we had played with, Pierre, spoke a little English and he said he had seen us with Dave at the marina earlier. So we started talking, with Tristan helping translate, and I asked Pierre what he knew about Dave Andrews. And whoa, Auntie! Wait till you hear!"

"I hope I don't have to wait much longer," Renie growled, watching her niece tie her shoes and settle back on the yellow cushions.

"Get this. Dave is the black sheep of a veddy veddy upper-crust family in England. He had an affair with the wife of a Member of Parliament—an older woman—and when he was caught with her, he soon disappeared with a fortune in jewels, her jewels. No one knows whether he stole them or she gave them to him. They couldn't prove anything because the woman committed suicide—over him! Dave was banished. He never has visitors from England, never talks about his family or his past. Well, of course he wouldn't."

Renie stared, aghast.

Twila grinned, then became serious. "Is this rich, or what? You'll have to watch it, Auntie Ren. He's a playboy black sheep and a criminal."

"I don't believe a word."

"I can see why you wouldn't want to."

"It's a ridiculous story. What did Tristan say about this?"

Twila hugged her knees. "Actually he didn't say a word about it. Not a damn thing, no comment. And then later he kept laughing about something, and I think he was laughing because now he knows about good old buddy Dave. Did you notice how he broke up when I goaded Dave about the jewels?"

It was true that Dave was trying to disengage himself from his past. True that he seemed to have severed all ties with England. True that he seemed to have all the money he needed. But this . . . it didn't fit the man she knew.

Hell, Renie thought. *What do I really know about him, except that he is incredibly handsome, and his voice and his eyes would render any woman helpless?* And he wrote children's fantasy tales. And something he couldn't or wouldn't talk about made him very sad. And if he wasn't falling in love with her, he was the best actor in the world.

She picked up one of the Wizard's books.

"Will you play dumb or confront him about this?" Twila wanted to know.

"I'll confront him, of course. I'll simply ask if it is true. It's a wild story, Twila, probably grossly exaggerated. Did this guy...what's his name?"

"Pierre."

"Did Pierre tell you how he found out all this, when even Tristan didn't know?"

"No. But maybe Tristan did know and didn't want to spill the beans."

"Or maybe it's just gossip. Sounds like gossip to me."

"Of course it's gossip. Of the juiciest kind. Why don't you go to dinner with us and confront him then? I want to watch."

Renie sighed. She ought to be more upset than she was about this. It just didn't seem right. "You know I can't keep late hours eating and drinking. Not while I'm in training."

"Dave still doesn't know about the training?"

She shook her head.

"He probably thinks you're with another man."

"I can't help what he thinks." She rose dejectedly and went to the captain's cabin to change. She had twenty minutes of exercise to do before she donned the fishtail for her nightly workout.

"You're not going swimming tonight, are you?" Twila called after her. "It's starting to rain."

"Are you afraid I'll get wet?"

"You can't go out in the ocean in a storm!"

Renie pulled on her sweat suit. "It isn't a storm, it's just a lovely, quiet rain."

Twila stuck her head into the cabin, pity all over her face. "I hope you're not too disappointed. I hope you didn't like him too much."

"I love him," Renie said softly.

"Omigod. Oh, how awful! I'll help you get over it. I'll ask Tristan to introduce you to a Frenchman."

"Twila, please! Please don't help me anymore, I beg you."

DAVE SAT CHIN IN PALM on his garden terrace, looking at the view of the sea and the unnamed cove. Such a short time ago Renie had been here with him, gazing at the same view. Now she would be on the *Sandrine II*, getting ready to go into the sea. For some mysterious reason it was what she did every night.

He was haunted by it. How the devil did she change into a fish?

Fish or not, this afternoon she had been a woman, the most alluring woman he had ever met, who had kissed him passionately, her heart thundering against his chest. Now he would go to the cove again, because she would be there. But no longer a woman.

He felt like a fool, sneaking down the slope to the rocky shore to get a glimpse of her as a mermaid. He found himself both averse to and awed by her damned double life. This was something he could not live with. Morgan nudged his leg, clearly wanting to play.

Dave stood up suddenly. "I've had enough of this game!" he announced.

The dog looked up with hurt eyes.

"Oh, I didn't mean you, Morg. This thing with Renie is turning into a stupid game and I'm out of patience playing it! It's time for a confrontation. I'm going out there."

Morgan cocked his ears and stared at him quizzically.

Dave began to pace. He was going to lose her, anyway, he calculated. If confronting her on the rock caused her to disappear sooner from his life, it couldn't be helped. It was better than this game of trying to pretend he didn't know her secret. Anything was better than sneaking down to the cove with binoculars every night....

He could maneuver his rubber boat along the edges of the cove in the shadows of the cliff. The low, drizzling clouds would filter out most of the light of the setting sun and the rising moon; it would be darker than usual. There were two other islets between the one the mermaid usually chose and the curve of the north shore. He could row silently around the curve and then out to the islet nearest her, tie up the boat, and snorkel to her rock from there.

It would be tricky. He would have to surprise her to prevent her from fleeing at the sight of a swimmer.

Dave slapped his fist into his palm. "I can do this, Morgan!"

What the mermaid would say to him, he had no idea. What he would say to her was even more impossible to predict.

RENIE SWAM WITH EASE. It was no longer difficult to maneuver the twists and turns and flips in the water; her rigorous training had paid off. Even with the weight of the plastic and metal tail, she could swim from the yacht to the islet without exhaustion. She was ready for the challenge of the movie role.

Ready and impatient. If Bryan Milstrom didn't contact her by tomorrow, she was going to find him and confront him herself.

Twilight was quickly darkening into night because of the rainy skies. She reached the islet and pulled herself onto the rock easily, remembering how the first few times she'd had scarcely enough strength to do it. This particular maneuver would be required on screen and she had it down to perfection.

Her body was warm from the exercise, so she did not feel cold, the temperature of the water was still warm, as well. Renie took several deep breaths and lay down up on the rock. The sky had no stars. The glow of a rising moon shone behind a veil of clouds in the east. She closed her eyes, loving the soft mist of the rain upon her face, and thought about the man who had kissed her in a lovely French garden this afternoon.

Kissed her with such need and such passion that her body had gone numb, crazy, and her mind had spun.

Was Dave really a playboy who'd had an affair with a rich, older woman and then run away with her jewels? It didn't compute. And was Tristan such a rogue as to find the account vastly amusing?

Renie tried to think of Dave in that role. He was handsome enough. Wealthy enough. Mysterious enough. The story didn't match what he had told her about himself, though. Unless he'd lied. And also . . . there was the sadness.

And there were the Wizard's tales about the fearless Wandering Prince and his goblin enemies. Fierceness dominated those stories, but there was an underlying gentleness in them. An underlying morality. The author of those stories was not a cad.

Hardly. He was the prince.

She closed her eyes and felt the rain again; she remembered the taste of his kiss and the catch in his voice when he'd told her he was bewitched. Their strange conversation about fear and feelings. Dave was sincere, she knew it.

"Renie . . ."

She heard his voice as if in a dream.

For some seconds she floated on the dream. Until she felt something cold and wet on her arm.

She shrieked with fright and her eyes shot open.

Peering over the edge of the rock, inches from her face, was a fogged-over snorkel mask. A diver's powerfully muscled arms reached out and grabbed her wrist.

A scream of helpless terror froze in Renie's throat.

7

"RENIE! It's me! Dave!"

Dave?

Her pulse was throbbing out of control. It felt as though the blood had drained from her head, leaving her dizzy and weak. His voice was frighteningly strange. Not just because it came from behind a mask. He articulated each syllable as if he were talking to someone who spoke a language other than his own.

Too startled to utter a sound, she watched him pull off the mask and attempt to climb onto her rock. He slipped repeatedly on the green lichen, grimacing in pain as he lost his hold and his knee slammed hard against sharp barnacles. He was wearing French swimwear—a shockingly small bikini. Almost naked, puffing, slipping and cursing the lichen, he released her wrist and managed to pull himself up beside her.

Suddenly conscious of her bare breasts, Renie arranged her wet hair to cover them, Mermaid style. Her hands shook with fright, and under the fishtail her mummified knees had lost all feeling.

"Fancy meeting you here," he panted, settling next to her.

"Dave! What in hell do you think you're doing?"

He looked at her blankly. "That's all you have to say?"

"What do you want me to say? You sneak up on me and pounce like a kidnapper . . . and scare me half to death. How dare you!"

"I didn't mean to scare you." The blank, awestruck expression seemed frozen to his face.

"Didn't mean to scare me? Is that why you sneaked up and grabbed me?"

She was growing angrier with each passing second. So angry that the fact hadn't yet sunk in he was not supposed to know she was out here. "Where did you come from, anyway? Whatever happened to a girl's privacy?" she demanded.

Dave just sat there staring at her like an idiot. "I'm sorry I grabbed you. I couldn't take a chance of your getting away. I didn't know what you would do if I swam out here."

"What do you mean, get away? We're on a piece of rock! Just where do you think I would *go*?"

"Into the water." He absently wiped at the scratches on his leg, which were bleeding slightly. "I had to . . . I wanted to confront you about this."

Renie gritted her teeth and kept trying to keep her hair from slipping and exposing her breasts. "Confront me about *what*?"

"About *this!*"

"I don't know what the devil you're talking about. What childish behavior! Dave, why are you staring at me like that? You're scaring me."

"I'm not trying to scare you."

"What a lie! What a mean trick, startling me to death. Who told you? Twila told Tristan, no doubt. Of course. And Tristan told you."

"No one told me."

"Someone had to have told you, and Twila is the only one who knows."

Dave brushed his thick, wet hair from his eyes. He had made no more attempts to touch her. "No one told me," he repeated. "I saw you out here on the rock."

"You saw me? When?"

"Before we met. Obviously, I couldn't believe what I saw. You might sympathize with what that was like . . . seeing you. The next night I returned to the cliff and you were there . . . here . . . again. This time I had binoculars and I could see your face clearly. Then when I saw you on the pier . . . the same face . . . well, bloody hell, I've been a crazy man ever since."

He did not look at her as he talked. He was acting so weirdly, treating her so differently . . . and saying *what*?

Her response was hollow, like an echo. She could hear it, as if it belonged to someone else. "You've been watching me? Thinking I . . . thinking . . . ?"

"Thinking you would be out here, yes. And tonight I couldn't stand it anymore. So I came. Hoping you wouldn't slide into the sea and swim away, down to wherever it is mermaids come from, and I would never see you again."

"Omigod! You actually . . ." Renie began to sputter. The sputters became laughter. She fell back, flapping her tail wildly and laughing until tears streamed from her eyes.

"I hardly find it that funny," he said grimly when it began to look as though she would never stop.

"I can't believe it!" she hooted.

"*You* can't believe it? How do you think I feel? It was crazy enough seeing a mermaid, but then to have her turn into a beautiful woman who just walks into my life . . ." He looked at her. "How can you do it? How do you grow legs?"

"All this time . . ." she began and then was convulsed once again.

She struggled to get control of herself. "So you swam out here to capture a sea siren! And do what with her?"

"I don't want to do anything with you. Except talk."

He was gradually working up the courage, she noted, to look at her tail. Even this close, even if it were not growing dark, the tail would fool him. It would fool anyone, even under the scrutiny of a camera close up; it had been designed that way by experts with the latest technology.

"I won't swim off," she said.

"Won't you? You're a mermaid. I know mermaids don't exist, but here I sit with you. Damn it, will you please stop laughing! I don't see that my discovering you is so funny."

"I didn't plan on getting caught, you see."

Reluctantly he reached toward the tail, then pulled back. The fishy appendage clearly repelled him. "How does it happen?" he asked again. "Can you get rid of this thing at will?"

She was choking on giggles, using every thread of willpower just to talk. *Hang on, I'm an actress,* she reminded herself. *I'm an aspiring film star and I can do this!* "If you mean can I get rid of my fishtail right now in the moonlight, no, I can't."

He lowered his head into the bend of the arm, that rested on his knees. "I've begun to doubt my own sanity. I came out here because I had to. There are a thousand questions I have to ask you. Why do you call yourself an American? How is this thing possible? How can—?"

She touched his arm and said huskily, "I don't want to answer all these questions now. Besides, I have some interesting questions of my own—for you."

"What questions?"

He sounded impatient. She began. "Twila heard about you. About you having an affair with the wife of a Member of Parliament and getting caught with her and running to France with her jewels while she was committing suicide over you. That's a pretty sordid scandal, Dave."

He stared at her. "I hadn't heard that one."

"Is any of it true?"

He raised his eyes toward the rain. "No. None of it."

"Then why would someone say it?"

"People love telling stories about me. I don't know where the stories come from. Just small-town..." He stared at her tail. "Blast, who cares about stories? Here we are, sitting and carrying on a conversation as if...as if...this were normal..." He paused, scratching his head. "I don't believe I'm awake...."

Renie could understand the gossip. A man who looked like this, who did not talk about himself. It could happen. He was so unshaken by the story, barely concerned that she had heard it, so it likely was not true.

It would be easy to rescue Dave from his discomfort right now by telling him her tail was a fake. At first she had been too angry. Then she'd been incapacitated by her howls of laughter. Now...

Now it was too much of a joke not to play along. Maybe he would kill her later, when he found out, but with a setup as perfect as this, it was too great to spoil so soon.

"Mermaids can take human form in all the stories," Dave was saying. "Usually they play cruel tricks on mortals. Are you one of those?"

"I guess you'll have to take your chances." She chuckled. "I might be. So beware."

"What kind of bloody answer is that?"

"I'm trying to tell you that if you don't want to be around a mermaid, then you shouldn't be out here, having a conversation with one."

She felt his eyes on her. The night was beginning to close in, and it was getting cold on the rock, but Dave was making no move to leave.

"Who are you?" he asked softly. "Who are you really?"

"I told you. My name is Renée Lloyd. What else do you want to know?"

"Damn it! Will you put an end to your ridiculous game? I want to know about that . . . that appendage!"

"I won't tell you. Not just now, anyway."

She flapped the tail against the rock. The slap echoed through the watery air. Dave stiffened.

The drizzle lightened. She saw the man in silhouette against the gray sky. How powerfully built he was, like a statue, sitting nearly naked next to her. Renie remembered his kiss and her heart beat faster. That intense thing; that physical draw was frighteningly strong.

She had imagined seeing...touching...the muscles and curves of his body without his clothes. Now his body was exposed to her scrutiny as they sat close on an isolated dot in the sea, and Renie began to ache for his passion-fired kiss again.

It was as if he were talking to someone else...as if he didn't remember those moments when new love had risen like perfumed mist into the fresh garden air. Of course he would be different...seeing what she was now.

She touched his bare leg. "Dave...it wasn't my idea for you to come out here. But now that you are here, what are you going to do?"

He cleared his throat. "I came to find some answers, but you won't give me any."

"Maybe you're asking the wrong questions. Aren't you curious whether sea sirens are warm or cold to the touch?"

He placed his hand over hers. "You are surprisingly warm."

"There, you see? Don't prejudge." She ran her fingers along his thigh and drew closer to him. "In the legends, mermaids must seduce men."

"I know."

"Mortal men can't resist them. Isn't that true?"

"Quite true," Dave replied.

"Do you think you can escape me, then?"

He touched her face. "I don't want to escape."

"Of course you don't want to." She tilted back her head provocatively, inviting his kiss.

His warm breath mingled with hers and as their lips drew together. His kiss was soft, a bit doubtful at first, but Renie pressed her mouth tightly to his and circled her arms about his head, her fingers stroking the back of his neck.

Feeling wildly mischievous, wildly uninhibited, she was intoxicated by sensations of losing herself in him. It no longer mattered that she did not plan to want him. It only mattered that Dave believed she could—and would—seduce him.

She was his fantasy. The fantasy of all men. She was a love-starved siren with primal urges that had to be satisfied. Had to be obeyed. She was enchantment. She was danger.

She offered herself seductively to his embrace. He smoothed back her hair so he could feel her breasts against his bare chest. He touched her throat. His hands moved gently over her shoulders, then over her breasts.

Renie trembled.

His hands were no longer damp and cold. They were dry, warm, and caressed her uncertainly at first, but soon, finding her skin soft, he touched her tenderly. She felt less lust in his touch than wonder.

"Are you cold?" he asked, his voice barely audible over the humming of the sea that surrounded them.

"Not when you hold me. Your body is very warm."

His hands cupped her breasts. "I can't help touching you. Your skin is satin. What are you doing... deliberately doing... to me?"

"What do you think?" Her fingers moved covetously down the length of his arms to the hands that cupped her, she tilted her face upward and closed her eyes. His lips responded.

Soft raindrops fell upon their shoulders. The tide lapped like an echo against the rocky edges of the islet, somehow sounding louder at dusk than in the brightness of day. The sea grew blacker, wrapping its million secrets in a heavier cloak of mystery. The water seemed depthless at night, its every shadow menacing.

"It's raining," she whispered, suddenly frightened; her passion was soaring far out of control. The rain was like a warning, a damper. "I have to go."

"I don't want you to go."

"I have to, Dave." *I can't let this go on,* she thought, desperate. *I don't know where to stop. He thinks I'll seduce him and I can . . . I will . . . if I stay.*

"No. You don't have to go," he said. "Stay with me."

Gently she pulled away. "I don't want to stay on a cold, wet rock."

"Then we'll go somewhere else." He raised his head in the direction of the yacht's lights.

"Twila is waiting for me. And for Tristan. Remember?"

This remark jolted him back to reality, something he did not want.

Neither did she. Caressing his thigh, she whispered, "I don't dare stay here . . . with moonlight shining on your wet body. . . . I can see in moonlight . . . I can see how you want me when you kissed me . . . when you touched my breasts. . . ."

Dave's fingers brushed through her damp hair. "I can take you to where the sand is soft and still warm from the heat of the day," he said hoarsely. "Will you lie with me on the ocean sand at the edge of the tide?"

"Is there such a place among those rocks?"

He pointed toward the shore. "Look at the silhouette of the coastline just straight across from the Sandrine. Do you see where it bends in sharply and then back out? There is a sand-bottomed cave in those rocks that's accessible only from the sea. I've ducked in there during dives sometimes. It's dry except when there's a storm tide. We'll go there."

"Funny I've never seen it," she said. "It's very close to the yacht."

"You wouldn't see it without being right there, because the rocks conceal it."

"Can you swim that far?" she asked.

"Of course I can. But we don't have to. I've a rubber boat tied to that nearest islet."

Renie laughed. "Can you picture me trying to get into a rubber boat?"

"I'll lift you. I'll carry you."

She slid off the rock and he followed. The water felt colder than before. Renie began to swim vigorously but, hampered by the weight of the tail, she could not keep up with him.

His curiosity, about her, about these strange and unexplainable moments of time, was insatiable. He attempted halfheartedly to find some hold on reality and couldn't. When they reached shore and sand . . . what would he learn about her then?

The dark sea sparkled. He did not know how it could, because the moon was so timid tonight, but there were sparkles around him like jeweled netting. Was it her magic?

"How deep can you go?" he asked, circling back to her in the ink-black water. "How long can you hold your breath?"

"Longer than you can," she answered, making a shallow dive, sending out more sparkles like a spray of fireflies.

Once in the rubber boat, he took a blanket from a seabag and threw it over her shoulders.

Renie sat balanced uncomfortably with her tail hanging over the edge and the filmy fins flopping in the breeze. *I must be out of my mind,* she thought. *But I've never had this much fun in my life! Someday I'll tell my grandchildren about the night I was a mermaid . . . but I won't tell them all of it. . . .*

The masquerade delighted her. She had no idea of how far she ought to carry the deception before it got plain mean. *Mermaids play cruel tricks.* Hell, Dave knew that! He was prepared for a mermaid's tricks and willing to take the risk.

The cold swim had done nothing to cool her rising passion thinking about him. Was she only imagining the sea sparkling all around them? Was she only imagining that when he touched her the night grew soft and hazy?

At the cave he got out and pushed the raft onto the sand. Renie wrapped herself tighter inside the blanket as he bent to lift her, because the sharp edges of the paper-thin metal scales could inflict cuts on his arms.

Handing her the flashlight, he carried her with ease, ducking into the cave entrance. The beam of light slashed erratically at the walls until he laid her up on soft, dry sand; now she shone it at the low ceiling and the wet, shiny sides of the cave. It was a tiny enclosure, hardly larger than a king-size bed, but cozy, well protected from wind and ocean spray.

She moved the light slowly, provocatively, over his body as he knelt above her. The suit he wore, a popular style on the Riviera, was tight and remarkably brief. His body was solid and well muscled, perfectly proportioned and thoroughly tanned.

He smiled at her without false modesty. "Do you like what you see?"

"Very much."

"Good."

"I won't ask the same question of you. I've noticed you avoid touching my tail."

"It takes some getting used to, I'm afraid."

"You haven't called me by my name, either. Do I seem like someone else to you?"

"How couldn't you? Yet you are the same. It's very confusing."

"I understand."

"I wonder if you do," he said sadly. He moved closer. "Renie..."

She could tell he'd forced himself to say her name because he was still wondering who...and what...she was.

"Renie...one moment I think I can't stand it unless I know about you, and the next moment I don't even care.... You've cast a spell on me and I don't care." He

Get 4 Books FREE

SEE BACK OF CARD FOR DETAILS

bent to kiss her. "You've caught me in your net of enchantment . . . sprinkled stardust in my eyes. I'm sure you are an illusion."

"Starlight illusions are made of magic," she said. "In tomorrow's sunlight the illusion will be gone."

"Then may tonight last forever."

She wrapped her arms about his neck. "Does that mean you can accept me like this?"

"I have no choice, have I? The truth is, your beauty astounds me as much tonight as it did this afternoon in the garden. Your lips taste as sweet. And your heart beats just as crazily against mine."

He stretched out beside her and kissed her chin and lips, then opened the blanket and kissed her neck and shoulders. His hands moved lightly over her breasts and his lips followed, raining feather kisses over her. He took the light from her and shone it over her body as she had done to him.

"You are beautiful," he muttered. "Lying there with your hair spread out under your head like a pillow of gold."

"I am your captive. . . ."

"You are my illusion."

"Kiss me again," she commanded, reaching up to him. "Kiss me the way you kissed me in the garden. Kiss me dangerously."

He put down the light, lifted her into a sitting position and held her against his chest, pressing his open mouth over hers as hungrily as before.

Renie devoured the taste of him and each of his quickening breaths. His tongue upon hers, his hands moving over her breasts, their bodies began to move in a primitive, erotic rhythm. The tiny cave filled with the sound of their breathing and the haunting, wanton song of Eros.

"This could soon become excruciating torture," Dave mumbled, clinging to the kiss between words, between breaths.

She knew exactly what he meant. It was becoming torture for her, as well, encumbered as she was by the stupid fishtail. But if she told him now, it would throw him so hard, it would shatter the most magical moment of their lives. If she encouraged him to try to help her out of the damned thing, he would rip it. Twila had been carefully trained for the job of peeling it from her body without damage to its thousand paper-thin scales. And even if she were to get it off here in the cave, the problem of getting it safely back to the yacht was too much of a risk.

"Renie . . . what's wrong?"

"What do you think?"

"I think you want me as much as I want you . . . but unless there's something important I don't know, a man cannot make love to a mermaid."

"That's true . . . in the conventional sense," she whispered. "But a mermaid can make love to a man."

8

DAVE'S EMOTIONS were out of control and he knew it. Mermaids wove magic and dangerous webs, and he was caught in one, not even trying to get out. It was too late to get out. As his eyes adjusted better to the darkness of the cave, with only the beam of light shining from the rock floor where the flashlight lay, he could see the shine in Renie's eyes. They shone with the dew of passion.

The part of him that believed in magic welcomed the mermaid in his arms; it was the sparkling of an illusion. His imagination throve on enchantment. "A mermaid can make love to a man," she had whispered in the strange, dim light that turned her pale skin a ghostly white.

"A mermaid's seduction is said to be a deadly and dangerous thing," he said huskily, stroking her long hair.

"Are you afraid of me?"

"No."

"Why not?"

"Because I don't believe in mermaids."

"Neither do I," she said. "Everyone knows the concept is an impossibility. You do know that, Dave."

"Of course I know that." He cupped her hands in his and kissed her fingers one at a time, sucking gently at first, then less gently at her fingertips. She brought their clasped hands to her mouth, moved her tongue along his fingers and closed her eyes.

He kissed her. Swimming in the fire of that kiss, he ached to press his body against hers, to feel warmth against his thighs, but could not. Touching the fishtail was more than he could stand. He buried his hands in her long hair and kissed her neck, moaning with frustration.

"Renie...make love to me...."

She gazed deeply into his eyes. "Dave..."

"What? What is it?"

"You're...you're making me want you so...this is completely out of hand...."

"Make love to me," he repeated. "Just...love me..."

Her fingers methodically explored his face, as if she were afraid she would miss some detail of his features, much as he had done earlier. The sensation of her fingertips moving gingerly over his face and throat and then along the contours of his chest was like being teased with hot ice.

Her breathing and the mist in her eyes told him she was as aroused as he, yet he sensed some hesitation in her, something slightly wrong.

"I'm not afraid of your spell," he assured her.

"Did it ever occur to you that I might be afraid of yours?" she whispered.

"I have no magic."

"Ah, but you do...like Elfin Prince does.... Is he capable of falling in love?"

"He is in love...with a beautiful mermaid."

Renie's breathing quickened. "And does she love him?"

"Yes."

He looked into her eyes. "Touch me, Renie...."

He guided her hands over his body. Her touch became electric; sparks shot through him. There was little question in his mind that she possessed some kind of unnatural power; never in his life had he experienced this helpless sensation of being out of control with passion. What was worse, he was unable to deal with the passion in the ways he knew.

He lay down beside her, guiding her hand lower, and closed his eyes at the first fire sparks of her intimate touch.

"Dave..." she whispered again, as if there was something she wanted to say to him. But seconds passed and she didn't say it. Instead her breathing quickened and she began to caress him.

The elastic top of his suit, which was becoming much too tight, uncomfortably so, caught between her fingers.

"When I saw you in this tiny French bikini..." she whispered "...almost naked..."

He raised his hips and slipped it off. "Is that better?"

"Yes...."

He closed his eyes again and let himself swim in the waves of heat that rippled from her hands. So many thirsting nights before her... and now her touch...

Buoyant yearning lifted him far above and beyond the moment when Renie touched him. The ripples of heat kept him afloat in a time he could not measure— didn't want to measure.

Just time, caught in a web of magic.

Her long hair began to tickle his skin like an assault of the softest feathers. The brushing of her hair... the warmth of her breath... the burning of her lips...

Dave floated in the blur until the pleasure of her seduction wildly awakened him to the intensity of her power. Her name formed in his throat and emerged as a quivering, rushing breath. He lay back in utter helplessness.

When he opened his eyes he could see rainbows on the ceiling of the cave. They couldn't be there, but he saw them nonetheless in the feverish heat of Renie's love.

He heard words forming inside his head... words rising from his heart... words he believed but could not speak... *Renie... I don't know you... I can't know you... but I love you....*

None of them came aloud from his throat. Helpless moans, sounding through the watery silence, were his only voice.

His body grew tense. He writhed, unable to lie still under her spell. There seemed to be shadows of sea waves undulating across the rainbows, and soon he was immersed in the rising and falling of the waves, caught and held in their unalterable rhythm.

How well she knew the needs dammed up within him... *how well she knew....*

Lurching, pitching, Dave's emotions surged to the bursting point. A great billow suddenly washed over him, without enough warning. He trembled violently and groaned.

Around his thighs he felt Renie's arms, holding him tightly against her body.

Ebb and flow of the tides. Ebb and flow of heated blood moving through his body. Gradually the tremors left him and he lay wrapped in her warmth, caught in a weighted net of love. In the euphoric afterglow, his thoughts filtered round his head like butterflies, airborne, with no place to land. *She is no myth. She is flesh.*

His fingers were entwined in her hair. He stroked in a circular motion, letting the gold flow between his fingers, until she roused and with a deep, ragged sigh, as if from a dream, wriggled about until she was where she wanted to be, lying in the bend of his arm, her head on his chest.

They lay listening to the echo of the lyrical song of the sea.

At length he said softly, "You are unbelievable. The most beautiful . . ."

"I hope you weren't about to say beautiful creature," she said lazily. "I don't take 'creature' as a compliment. I take it literally."

"I wasn't going to say it," he said. But he wasn't entirely sure that was true.

"Tonight," she whispered, "I was a slave to my creature emotions. I don't know what you do to me. For awhile there I was your slave."

Dave smiled. "Am I the only man alive who has a mermaid as a lover?"

"No question about it," Renie said sleepily. Lying on his chest, she began again to hum the same haunting tune, the one he had first heard in the car when they drove along the coast.

Her tousled hair tickled his throat and chin. He tasted salt in her hair.

"Renie, you have to explain it to me."

"Explain what?"

"You know what."

"I will," she promised insincerely.

"Explain it to me now."

"Now?" Her voice suddenly rose to a high, cracking pitch. "Now? Oh, Lord, not now, in this beautiful . . . Oh, what time must it be?" She rose on one elbow. "I can't stay here any longer! I'm hideously late, and Twila is going to be so frantic, she'll be calling out the harbor patrol to look for me. She'll think I drowned!"

"How the devil could you drown?"

"Never mind how. Honestly, Dave, I'm panicking. I told you before, on the rock, that Twila expects me back. I have to get to the boat. Please help me! I can barely move in the stupid, damned fishtail. Oh, curse! I've just rolled on the flashlight! Where is that thing?"

In a moment the light flashed on again. "At least it still works," she said, directing the beam and trying to untangle herself from the blanket.

"One would think you'd be more adjusted to your . . . tail, after wearing it for centuries," Dave muttered as he groped about the shadowy cave, looking for his swimsuit.

"Could you adjust to a thing like this?"

"I don't . . . think so." He found the suit and pulled it on. "How do you know you can trust me not to reveal your secret to anyone?"

She laughed. "I'm not worried. Who would listen to you?" She arranged herself on the partially folded blanket. "My scales are sharp. I wouldn't want you to cut yourself carrying me to your boat. I have to be careful not to damage my tail on the rocks."

Dave wished she would stop talking about her tail, yet was eager for any bits of information. He lifted her, ducking through the cave entrance, and deposited her gently in the rubber boat while she held the flashlight in front of them.

"Oh, do please hurry," she pleaded.

The rain had stopped, and through an opening in the clouds the moon was visible. It shone full and bright over a small patch of sky that opened like a three-dimensional picture. One star glittered like a diamond just below the moon.

The *Sandrine II* was anchored not far away. As he rowed toward her lights, Dave's eyes adjusted to the darkness so that he could see Renie's lovely face. Her skin was so white, her eyes and her lips were so pale, she appeared fragile, but he knew she was not. Her hair caught reflections of moonlight, and mystically, the light of that sparkling, single star.

"Twila will be on vigil on the afterdeck," Renie said. "Don't get close enough for her to see you."

"Why not?"

"Because she'll . . . because it was selfish and spontaneous, my staying so long with you. She'll get angry, and that strained, mad look will stick on her face for hours. Unless Tristan is able to find a way to sweeten her up. They'll jump to all sorts of conclusions about what we...were up to. I'd rather explain to her in a calmer atmosphere, not when I've made her late for her date. I hate turmoil and tantrums. Just please drop me into the water and I'll swim in."

"Whatever you want."

"This is far enough, actually," she said, pushing the blanket away. "I'll slide off here."

He halted the oars and moved forward to kiss her. The ocean was dark and silent; it murmured reminders of their sharing. Her warmth was still on his skin.

"About tonight," he whispered. "I will never forget tonight."

"Neither will I." She smiled as she spoke.

She held out her hands to him. He felt something cool and smooth in his palm.

"A seashell?"

"Yes. A memento of tonight...a little gift of love from a mermaid."

Dave's fingers folded around the memento from her world. "It might as well be made of gold," he said. "The moments with you...memories of you...have made me rich."

"Priceless memories for us both," she said.

He squeezed her hand. "Tomorrow?"

"Sure. I'll meet you at the marina again. That is, unless I hear about my job and can't make it. In case that happens, and I can't manage to get hold of you, don't wait more than ten minutes."

"I half expect you to change your mind and disappear."

"Why?"

"Because mermaids do things like that."

"I'm not a real mermaid. I'm just a . . . novice."

"You're a what?"

Renie gave him a quick peck on the cheek and said, "I'll dream of you tonight."

Before he could answer, she had slid gracefully from the boat and into the sea. He saw the gleam of her hair in the moonlight before she disappeared completely into the shadows of the waves.

He waited a few moments. Now, he began to feel the chill of the night air. He pulled a sweatshirt from the bag under his seat and slid it over his head. A surprisingly short time elapsed, then he heard the shouting of women's voices from the *Sandrine II*. Renie was safely home.

Dave knew his concern for her safety didn't make much sense. The ocean at night was filled with sparkles and echoes and predators of the deep, but a mermaid was herself part of the ocean. A daughter of Neptune would know the night sea as well as he knew the woodland paths of his childhood.

Wouldn't she?

What did she mean, she was a novice? What kind of remark was that?

Gradually he became aware that his left knee was bleeding, cut by her sharp scales. The cut was welcome proof that tonight had really happened. Like the seashell in his hand.

Rowing back, he thought, *She probably won't be there tomorrow. She gave me tonight, but tomorrow is too much to ask for.*

She's already a memory, he decided, clutching the treasure from the sea that she had given him.

ON BOARD, at the table in the galley, Twila handed Renie a cup of sweetened, steaming coffee. "I was about to call out the French Foreign Legion!"

"I doubt if the French Foreign Legion would have come," Renie said mildly. "Camels are useless in the ocean." She had already apologized three times, with genuine guilt.

"I kept thinking about sharks." Twila shuddered. She had talked about sharks at least once a day since they arrived on the French coast. Renie had yet to see one.

"I did tell you I was more tired than usual," she answered. "You must have considered I might fall asleep on the islet."

Twila pursed her lips. "How could you possibly fall asleep, half-naked on a rock in the rain?"

Renie sipped the coffee and didn't reply. Her mind was so full of thoughts of Dave, she was only half listening. Her emotions were torn between guilt at having deceived him and a sense of wonderful, wild adventure. The guilt was not very strong because it had all been so good. He believed a mermaid had made love to him.

Still, no man appreciated being made to look foolish. Was he going to think she had deliberately tried to make a fool of him? That she was laughing at him?

I think I've been bad, she scolded herself. It had been fantastic, making love to him. How easy it was to love him! And how easy it might be to lose him when he discovered her stupid little trick.

Renie sighed sadly. It had been a long time since she had cared about any man. Love had never worked for her. This man filled her every waking thought and goaded her every fantasy. She loved him far more than she wanted to; love came with the risk of awful pain. She loved him . . . yet she had dared push his love to the limit by deceiving him.

Dave . . . her heart whispered. *Dave, I'm sorry.* . . .

"Auntie Ren, are you there? Twila to Auntie. Hello?"

"What?" Renie asked.

"Don't you want your messages? Bryan Milstrom phoned that he will arrive sometime tomorrow afternoon. They're driving down from Paris with a van full of equipment. So they're ready to begin."

Renie's heart lurched. She set down the coffee cup. "He must have said more than that."

"Yes. He wants to meet with you around six in the evening. He said he would take the marina taxi and come out here."

"Omigod. What do you think it means, his coming here to the boat?"

"I think it means you got the job."

"He would talk to me even if I didn't get it, Twila. And in private, because that's the sort of man he is."

Twila rested her hand on Renie's. "I don't know why he didn't just tell me what the decision is. Why do they play these stupid games? I'm trying to remember verbatim. He said his office won't be set up for another couple of days. He was in a rush, and didn't stay long on the phone. Honest to God, Auntie, I think they would have told you sooner than this if the contract wasn't going to go to you. After all, Bryan gave you their precious tail to use, didn't he? He has the greatest faith in you."

Renie nodded, believing Twila's reasoning. She smiled and said, "You have a date with Tristan. Where is he?"

"Not here yet, thank God. I was afraid he was going to be here to witness you being hauled aboard, flapping your tail." Drumming her nails on the tabletop, she gazed out of the window toward the harbor. "Tristan ought to be here by now."

Getting up to refill her coffee mug from the pot on the stove in the galley, Renie said, "The reason I was late is that I've been with Dave for the past hour and a half. He swam out to my rock, if you can believe it."

Twila drew in her breath. "What?"

"It seems he has seen me out there for several nights. He thinks I'm a mermaid."

The look of astonishment on Twila's face was transformed into amusement. She dissolved into peals of laughter.

"It's worse than you think," Renie said. "I didn't tell him otherwise. He still thinks it."

"He couldn't!"

"How could he not? What else was he supposed to think when he saw me?"

Twila, still laughing, rose and began to pace wildly around the cabin. "You're *wicked!*"

You don't know half how wicked, Renie thought. But she had no intention of revealing the rest.

"Just please don't say anything to Tristan. Dave will be furious enough, learning the truth from me. If he hears it from somebody else first, it'll be even worse."

"I don't blame you for wanting to see his face when he finds out what a fool he is!"

"Actually, Twila, I don't think I do."

The giggling stopped for a few seconds, and then Twila started again. It was catching. Renie couldn't hold back laughter of her own. It was all so crazy and bizarre.

"So you were playing your role...practicing your role as a sea creature. Oh, this is rich! What on earth did the two of you talk about? What the devil did he say? What did you say?"

"Naturally he was full of questions. Which I tried to fend off. Mainly he was afraid I'd swim away." She pulled the towel from her still-wet hair. "He couldn't bring himself to touch the tail. The more I laughed, the tighter that damned costume felt."

"It serves him right for lying to you about his past. I'm glad you got him, Auntie. The guy has made a career of immoral affairs and using women for his own gain, then tossing them away. You did good, making a fool of him."

"He didn't lie to me about his past. I asked him about the story and he said it wasn't true."

"Did you expect him to admit it? I'm having a hard time picturing this—a conversation between a man and a fish. In the dark in the rain on a wet, slimy rock."

They saw the lights of a small boat approaching from the direction of the shore.

Twila rose and began to search for her sweater. "It's hilarious!"

"I'm going to the other cabin to dry my hair and read," Renie said. "I don't feel like talking to Tristan.

Just please don't drink too much and get to giggling about this in front of him. Promise me."

"Me? Do such an irresponsible thing as tell Tristan you are not a creature of the deep?"

Armed with a hot drink and the borrowed volumes of *The Wizard's Fireside Tales*, Renie propped herself on pillows in her bunk. Memories of the night caused a smile to form on her lips and warmth to rush through her blood. She thought of the feel of Dave's body, the hard muscles of his chest. His silhouette in the smoky light of the cave. His voice. The touch of his hands. The fiery touch of his lips....

She leaned back and closed her eyes, luxuriating in the memory of his feel, his taste.

He's in love with the mermaid, Dave had said of the Wandering Prince. *He's in love....*

She picked up the book and gazed dreamily at its cover. The eyes of the Prince of Lost Clouds were silver blue, like Dave's....

TWILA SHOOK HER vigorously. "Auntie Ren! Wake up! I have something to tell you!"

Renie stirred and winced at the cabin light shining in her eyes. "What time is it?"

"It's nearly three o'clock. I just got back. But I couldn't wait until morning to tell you what I found out about Dave!"

A wave of panic went through Renie's body. *He has told someone.*

Groggy, she sat up and stared at Twila in horror. "He didn't! He couldn't have!"

Her niece shook her again. "You're not awake yet. Come on. Wait till you hear this!"

"For Godsake, what?"

"Dave has amnesia!" Twila took off her sweater and began to undress. "That's why he never talks about England. He doesn't remember anything. He is an ex-race-car driver. His car wrecked during a championship race in Germany, and he was horribly hurt—head injuries that left him with amnesia."

Renie said nothing, merely stared.

"It's true."

"For this you woke me at three in the morning? You promised you wouldn't get smashed."

"I'm not smashed. You can tell I'm not." Twila was now in her underwear, tripping over her panty hose as she tried to get out of them. "Tristan and I ran into someone from Dave's village."

"Again?" Brushing her tousled hair from her eyes, Renie squinted at her niece. "Isn't this getting a little ridiculous?"

"But it explains everything, don't you see? Maybe bits and pieces of his memory come out now and then and the story of his life gets pieced together."

"Only yesterday he was a thief."

"Yeah, he seems to have had quite a busy life. A little amnesia doesn't slow him down much."

"He doesn't have amnesia," Renie said, sliding back between the blankets.

"Of course he does. It's obvious. Amnesia explains everything."

Renie yawned. "What did Tristan have to say?"

Twila was in her pajamas now. She sat on the edge of the berth that stretched across the width of the bow, bulkhead to bulkhead. "Tristan finds it highly amusing."

"But he didn't *say* anything?"

"No."

Dave's body had no scars, Renie reflected. Not that scars meant anything. She believed Dave's denial of Twila's last wild story. He would probably deny this one, too. He was a London businessman before he came to the south coast of France; he had told her so. London businessmen could be race-car drivers with amnesia, she supposed. It could be true.

But not likely. Dave Andrews was a man who was trying to forget his past, not remember it.

9

THE FOLLOWING MORNING Dave was busy at his desk, when Morgan rose with a shrill bark from his nap on the rug and ran to the front door.

"Bonjour, Davey!" Tristan called from the foyer. "What are you doing?"

"Working. Come in."

"Working on what?" Tristan, petting the dog, walked into the room and stood behind Dave's chair, reading the sentences on the computer screen. "What's this about a Fir Bolg goblin hunter and a mermaid?"

"The latest of *The Wizard's Fireside Tales,*" Dave answered, surprised that the Frenchman had decided to visit his house.

Tristan picked up the top page of a pile of manuscript papers from the desk and read slowly.

"A tribe of water trolls, led by a lovesick lost elf, looking for a mermaid? *Mmm, oui.* I see. So this is a sample of the brilliant workings of an Englishman's mind. The mind upon which hangs the most important conviction of terrorists in the western world. The mind upon which I am gambling my reputation. This is cause for alarm!"

Dave grinned. "You and the Fir Bolg Soldier are both inclined to be too quick to alarm." He shuffled the papers to find a sketch of the Fir Bolg. "Look how rigid he is and never a smile. But at least his faith in the bungling prince stays firm."

Tristan gazed at the yellow-haired, puffy-faced Fir Bolg, who was wearing cowboy boots that reached halfway up the length of his tiny legs. "What in hell are you rambling about? And who is this W. W. Wizard?"

"You wouldn't expect me to use my real name, would you? Do you want coffee?"

"But of course. I would not have come all the way up the hill unless I knew you had coffee."

While Dave went to the kitchen, Tristan remained beside the desk, looking over the rest of the manuscript.

When Dave returned with a small cup of strong coffee, Tristan glanced up with a grin. "This three-fingered goblin Fireskog is quite amusing."

Dave nodded. "The three-fingered man in my nightmares is not amusing. Do you know how frustrating and how helpless it feels to know those bastards blew up a plane . . . and be powerless to do anything about it? The anger's eating me alive. These books are an outlet for my rage."

Tristan said softly, "Fireskog and Grig Goblin seem indestructible."

"I'll do them in well and thoroughly at the end of the series."

The Frenchman set down the pages upon the cluttered desk and accepted the coffee.

"Perhaps your wandering prince will conquer them sooner rather than later. I am getting rumbles from my network that you've been spotted."

Dave felt himself start to perspire. "How? By whom?"

"There is no way of knowing by whom. The history of every passenger on that plane has been investigated thoroughly. I have always worried that someone—either police or terrorist—would root out the man from whom you bought your fake passport. Any investigation would reveal that you were carrying a great deal of cash."

Dave felt anger rise without knowing why. Was he angry with Tristan for not having better information? With himself, for being so stupid as to be in this predicament in the first place? Letting it burst out, he demanded, "What do you mean, you're getting rumbles? Don't you have any dependable information?"

"I'm trying to get it, *mon ami*. So far no information is confirmed about your being spotted, but if I were you, I would begin to think about returning to England."

"When did you hear this ... unconfirmed information?"

"I phone Paris every morning."

"If I go back, I'll be walking into prison."

"You'll be walking into worse if these terrorists find you before the authorities do."

"It isn't urgent yet."

"Probably not. But I believe it is only a matter of time, perhaps a very short time. Where there is smoke there is fire."

Dave turned off his computer. "I have a loaf of bread in the kitchen," he said.

When they were seated at the wooden table in front of the kitchen window, with the morning sun streaming in and the sound of the birds in concert in the garden, Tristan smiled mischievously. "Why should I not be quick to alarm when my witness has amnesia?"

"Amnesia? Who?"

"You don't remember? You have been a race-car driver, now suffering from amnesia. Oh, but of course, you would not remember...." He sipped his coffee and laughed. "What a magnificent past you have, *mon ami*."

"Not more stupid rumors?" Dave set a dish of butter and some jam upon the table and began slicing the bread.

"*Oui*. It is the latest story they're telling about you in the village. And only yesterday a young man called Pierre told Twila and me you're a jewel thief. Do you know a Pierre?" He chuckled. "They tell wonderful stories about you, Davey! Why is this? Surely you don't spread your goblin tales around the village?"

Dave laughed. "I have told them absolutely nothing. That's the reason for the stories. They think I'm deliberately secretive, so they make up stories to explain why."

"You're aware of this gossip?"

"Yes. But not of the extent of it. Why would they be talking to you about me?"

"Why not? I am more one of them than you are. Besides, Twila digs for information like a sand crab. I think she wants Renie to know the sort of man she's involved with."

Dave buttered a slice of bread. "I doubt whether Renie would care much one way or the other what I am."

Eyebrows rose. "What does that mean?"

"Just what I said. She's an independent woman who makes her own judgments."

The Frenchman grinned. "Ah, surely you are lovers, you and this woman you wanted to know better."

"Here," Dave suggested. "Have some jam."

Tristan helped himself and leaned forward, chewing. "Joking aside, this strange children's book of goblins and fairies . . . one would not dream you had such a side. You're still carrying around the daydreams of youth."

"Guilty as charged. Adulthood isn't any fun."

"Do you have children of your own? Did you leave children behind in England?"

"No. I'd have mentioned it if I did."

"Would you? We were months into our comradeship before you mentioned your wife."

"It wasn't important."

"Most people think marriage is somewhat important."

"My marriage was falling apart. I told you that. My wife was also my business partner, and her marketing ideas were bankrupting the business."

The Frenchman wiped jam from his chin. "Why did you allow her to do that?"

"She was the daughter of my business partner, Frederick. When Frederick died suddenly, she inherited his sixty percent. Then my problems really started. The marriage went sour, the business was failing, my wife took a lover, and I got a bleeding ulcer." He helped himself to a second slice of bread. "I had a lot to escape from. But I wouldn't have deserted a child."

"Why have you never told me before precisely what you *did* run from?"

Dave looked at him incredulously. "Because we agreed that I wouldn't talk about my past. Remember?"

"Ah, of course. So why are you telling me now?"

"You asked, damn it."

"I did not ask as much as you told me," the Frenchman said gently. "You are different today. Something in you has changed. Something in you needs to talk. Forgive me for saying it, *mon ami*, but your eyes look very lonely today."

Tristan's personal observation angered Dave, but he responded honestly. "Well, I'm always lonely. It's the price of exile."

"*Oui*, that is so. Yet today I think it has to do with the beautiful American woman."

Dave was uncomfortable with Tristan's uncanny skill at reading him. Last night a mermaid's tender love had thrown him off balance. She was a reminder of the importance of loving and being loved. Now Tristan was making him think of children he had wanted and never had . . . probably never would have. . . .

A mermaid's physical love had left him empty. He knew he could never have her, because no man can "keep" a mermaid, but he loved her. Damn. He loved her. The loneliness overwhelmed him. He'd needed to talk today, even to Tristan, and Tristan was picking up on the difference in him.

A small breeze teased the sheer white curtains of the window. From outside came the fresh fragrance of greenery and flowers. Morgan was impatiently nudging Dave's leg, wanting his share of bread and butter and jam. Morgan, usually oblivious to anyone's feeling but his own, seemed to sense something was bothering his master this morning. He had followed him around without demanding a game of ball, and had actually jumped off the table when Dave yelled at him for barking at the neighborhood cats. Dave gave him a generous bite as his reward for being far less obnoxious than usual.

Tristan Escoiffier sipped his coffee and chuckled, watching Morgan lick jam from his pink and black nose. "You amaze me, Davey, truly you do. With these strange stories of make-believe...."

"Some of what we assume is make-believe isn't," Dave said.

"Why do you say that?"

"I know it to be true."

"Je ne sais pas." The typical Frenchman's shrug again. "I know nothing of make-believe. I have encountered only bitter reality."

"Yes. And for that, my good friend, I am sorry for you."

What would this man have done, Dave wondered, if he had been the one to spot the mermaid on the rock? Hunt her down with a net and sell her to the highest bidder?

RENIE WAS WAITING for him and she had legs again. He had never seen her legs except through the folds of her long skirt when the sun was at her back, but he imagined them to be long and beautiful. The sight of her sent Dave's emotions soaring. Memories of last night were hot and sharp, as though he had kissed her goodbye only moments ago, then watched her slide into the black water and disappear into the eerie shadows. With weak, watery moonlight on the soft roll of the tides . . . moonlight on her golden hair.

She was someone else then, last night. She was make-believe. Now she stood straight and tall before him and her hair was dry and blowing in the breeze under the brimmed hat she wore.

His incredible secret.

To his shock, she had come as she'd promised.

The traffic was sparse enough for him to stop at the curb while she got in. Renie greeted him with a smile that was different from the way she had smiled at him before. A private smile, for a lover.

He smiled back. "I wondered if Twila would be with you." He was glad she wasn't.

"Twila and Tristan have taken a ride in a speedboat. The last I saw of them, they went zooming off into the distance, waving at me. So we're alone."

"Good," he said.

"I told Twila I wanted to be alone with you this afternoon, so we could talk."

"So you can give me some answers?"

"Yes," she said hesitantly, pulling off her hat.

He could feel her eyes on him as he drove. "Where do you want to go?"

"To a nice, quiet little café, where we can talk over lunch."

Dave placed his hand over hers. "Now that I see you looking so beautiful…in the light…standing…I don't know which I want more—explanations of how you transform your body or . . ."

She waited and finally asked anxiously, "Or what?"

"Or you . . . as a woman."

"You want to make love to me as a woman?"

"I haven't thought of much else since last night. How could I think of anything else?"

"That's . . . good," she muttered, looking out the window at the road.

He drove in tense silence. "We left something unfinished."

"Yes."

"I don't know how to express my feelings for you," Dave said awkwardly. "Certainly I'm fascinated, but it's a lot more."

"You think I have placed a spell on you," she said softly.

"I know you have."

"I haven't, Dave."

"I still feel your touch, your lips…and my brain plays crazy tricks because I hear you singing when you're nowhere near."

The street was lined on one side with cypress trees. On the other a river tumbled from the mountains to empty into the sea. They had turned off the main thoroughfare, onto this narrower road that followed the curving riverbank. Dave pulled to the side of the road and turned off the engine.

"Renie, you seem very nervous. You're bothered by my curiosity about you. What are you thinking... and feeling after last night?"

She looked at him wistfully and did not smile. "You want to know why last night happened, don't you? You are unsure what motivated me, whether it was love or lust."

"I don't know how to separate you from the legends." He did not want to use the word "mermaid" in the light of day; it was as if doing so would break the spell of a night when mermaids had been real. In the light of day they were not.

"In the legends, mermaids are capable of falling in love," Renie said.

"Is it true?"

"Of course it's true."

Dave met her eyes. "You're speaking from experience."

"Last night's experience." Suddenly timid, she looked away. "I am impulsive, Dave. Impulsive and mischievous. I was caught up in the moment, and making love to you last night was very impulsive. But my feelings were not impulsive. I could not make love to a man unless my feelings for him were very strong. Is that what you are asking? It *was* lust, of course it was. It was also love."

He touched her lips lovingly with his fingertips.

"And you didn't have to ask," she added. "You knew."

Dave stroked the flyaway strands of her hair. "A man as baffled as I am isn't certain of anything."

"Not even of your own feelings? We haven't established whether or not a mortal is capable of loving a mermaid. I mean, maybe it is curiosity." She touched his arm. "Oh, I'm being so unfair. I really am. Why are we sitting here by the side of the road where it's so hard to . . . try to talk?"

"I don't know. I think I just wanted to look at you in daylight."

Her face flushed. "Where are we headed?"

"To a garden café at the edge of the peach groves. It has a fine view of the sea. Very private. We can have an aperitif in the garden and lunch."

Her nervousness was very evident now. He knew he had asked her questions she did not want to answer, now or ever. He wondered just how much about herself she was willing to reveal.

"Is it far?" she asked.

"Five or six minutes along the river. Do you have to be back early again?"

"Yes."

"To swim in the sea?"

"Actually, no. I have a business appointment."

Something beyond my comprehension is going on here, Dave thought. And whatever it was had to do with last night. Her seduction had been welcome. In spite of the legends about the fate of other "chosen" men, he only wanted more of her.

He turned onto a narrow side road that curved through peach groves and thick vegetation. The road widened into a parking area, on one side of which the red-tiled roof of the café showed through the trees.

Standing in the parking area, they could both smell and hear the river. New growth was sprouting from the rains of the autumn storms after the dry, hot summer. Jasmine was flowering sending perfume into the air to mingle with the fresh, wet scents of the river.

"It's beautiful here," Renie said. "We're very close to the riverbank. Can we walk down there?"

"If you like." Dave took her hand. He wasn't sure, but he thought he felt her trembling.

They followed a footpath, walking in silence until the grassy bank appeared in front of them.

Dave sat down on the grass under a tree and motioned to her to sit beside him. She sat close, her shoulder against his, gathering her skirt around her knees. He touched her legs, moving his hand in long strokes along her thigh to her knee, then to her ankles. Renie sat in silence and watched as he pushed up her skirt to touch her skin.

"Forgive my fascination with your legs," he said. "Such beautiful legs . . . such soft skin . . . I don't know how you are possible, Renie, and right now I don't care. Please just let me touch you."

"We were going to talk. . . ." she protested weakly.

"It can wait."

"Maybe it shouldn't. . . ."

"It can wait," he insisted, while his fingers explored the backs of her knees and her inner thighs.

The heat generated in his body merely by touching her flamed over him like fire. Waves of fire. He remembered last night, the intensity of her love. "I want you as a woman, Renie . . . I love you as a woman."

"You love the mystery," she said.

"No. I don't want the mystery. I want the woman."
Dave stroked her hair. The sunlight slanting through
the tree branches above and the small breeze turned the
wisps of her hair into silver-gold sparkles that shone like
runaway sunbeams.

"The magic of you is beyond earth...even beyond
sea," he whispered. "You have pulled me into your life
without so much as a struggle."

She touched his face affectionately. "Dave, I must
explain...."

"Please explain. But not right now. If we talk it will
break the spell."

"And the illusion," she said softly.

His lips were brushing hers. "You seem to think things
will be different if you explain the biology of mermaids."

"They will be."

"Why?"

"The magic will be gone."

"Then don't tell me...not yet...not now...not while
last night is still unfinished...."

One hand in her hair, his lips moved slowly over
hers. Renie opened her lips and welcomed his kiss.

"Let's go into the grove," he said. "If anyone should
come down here to the riverbank, the trees will hide
us." He grasped both her hands in his and rose, pulling
her up with him.

In the deep silver and blue shadows of the thick
copse, he kissed her again and urged her onto the soft,
sweet-smelling earth to lie with him.

"The desire to touch your legs is the strongest sexual urge I've ever felt," he said. "What beautiful legs you have. I want to love you the way I couldn't..."

There was no taste of salt in her hair or on her skin; only a fragrance like flowers. Her skirt billowed beneath her like a filmy blanket. His hands moved over the silk of her blouse. Over the lace briefs under her skirt. Her skin, pale and smooth as cream, must not touch earth, he determined, for there could be little thistles hidden in the darkness of the undergrowth. She was too delicate...too beautiful...too accustomed to the softness of the nurturing sea to be subjected to the nettles and thorns of his earth.

After he kissed her again, a long, deep kiss that caught a low moan in her throat, Renie said huskily, "You are the only man I've ever known who makes me afraid of myself."

"Don't be afraid. Don't ever be afraid of anything when you are with me."

"Yours are dangerous hands," she muttered. "But so warm...."

"The warmth is you. The pounding in my heart is you. The shortness of my breath is you."

She closed her eyes.

Dave sensed the fear she spoke of. His male reasoning, however, had difficulty with her explanation. If Renie was afraid, it must be of him. She felt fragile in his arms. He had not thought of her as fragile last night in the environs of the sea, but now she seemed so small and light, so vulnerable. He was aware of how much smaller she was than he.

A strong desire to protect her rose up in him . . . his powerful male instincts surfacing, too long unused.

He had been too long without love. Logic lost all shape and melted in the heat of her, like butter in sunshine. He could not control how he felt about Renie and knew it. He had known this last night, caught in the gauzy net of illusion.

He lifted her hand to his lips and kissed her fingers. In the filtered sunlight under the leaves he caressed her body.

"Let me love you, Renie," he whispered.

She looked at him with eyes full of love and dreams.

He stroked her under her skirt. Careful not to expose her to the elements of earth, but only to his touch, he slid off the lace. She could not lie still.

"You are . . . miracle. . . ." he whispered.

"I am not a miracle," she whispered back in fitful breaths. "I am only a woman."

"Miracle..." he sighed. "Soft...so moist...wanting me as much as I want you. . . ."

Her body quivered and tensed. She grasped his shoulders tightly and hung on, as if afraid of falling. When she closed her eyes, she saw the night sky and the stars and felt their prickling fires again, so intensely she thought she would die from the feeling. Silently she screamed his name again and again, giving his name to every star that shone upon her.

"Renie," he whispered, "I want to take you slowly, but I can't because today is the afterglow of last night and I'm still caught in it. I've waited too long for you. . . ."

"Don't wait," she begged, shuddering against him.

He removed his clothes and moved over her. Renie's moan of pleasure was music to him and filled him with fire. The music seemed to extend into the very air around them, filling the copse and mingling with the singing of the river.

They were one. His body absorbed the throbbing heat of hers. Her body melted into his heartbeats and the rhythms of his love. He looked into her blue eyes.

"I love you...." he breathed, trembling with a strong spasm of release.

The unfamiliar emotion surged and flowed from him to her . . . from his soul into hers.

"I love you," she cried, half breath, half moan. Her eyes were moist, her cheeks streaked with tears.

Still trembling, Dave brushed his lips across her eyes, tasting the salt of her tears. He knew in that moment that Renie's heart was the heart of a woman.

Had he a right to do this?

I have no right to her, he thought.

10

RENIE COULDN'T SLEEP. Bryan Milstrom had not only drawn up the contract, but had scheduled her to do a publicity film shoot in the mermaid costume the following afternoon. By the day after, the actual filming would begin. There would be no letup in the work during the coming four weeks unless autumn storms interfered.

And still Dave didn't know the truth. If he found out from someone else, he would be so humiliated that it would probably be the end of the romance right there. He would be justifiably furious. Why had she given in again to passion—his and her own—and let the lie go on?

Now her mischief could cause her to lose the only man she had ever really wanted.

And what a hell of a way to begin the most important job of her life; in an emotional turmoil over Dave Andrews and what she had done to him.

She had thought of phoning him after Bryan Milstrom left, but Bryan had stayed very late, talking about the project. His last words had had to do with her looking her best tomorrow for the photo shoot. If she got together with Dave after midnight to give him the jolt of his life, there would be no hope of sleep. The best plan was to get in touch with him in the morning and talk to him then.

But in the morning she couldn't reach him. Time after time she tried.

They started up the engine and moved the *Sandrine II* farther into the cove, near the north shore and very near the islet the photography director had selected for the publicity pictures.

Twila paced excitedly about the cabin, drinking champagne and talking about her favorite scenes from motion pictures, and raving about living in a dream.

Renie felt less like celebrating. She sat by the window, peeling an orange and looking at her watch every few minutes. "The makeup person is due anytime," she said. "And I'm supposed to be meeting Dave in less than an hour. Where the devil could he be? Probably working on some motor somewhere. Twila, you've got to meet him for me and explain that I can't make it."

Twila waved her glass. "Me? I can't leave. You need me here."

"There will be more people than I want to help me get ready for this. When I need you is after the photo thing is finished and I have to get aboard and out of the tail. It wouldn't take you that long to meet Dave and give him the message and then putt on back here."

"You want me to break the news to him that you're a film star?"

Renie dug viciously at the orange. "Just be careful what you say, though, Twila. I have a lot to talk to Dave about. He stills thinks I'm a mermaid."

"What?" Twila stopped pacing and plopped onto a chair at the table opposite Renie.

"I was going to tell him yesterday and then I didn't. Well, actually, he didn't want me to. Not at this time. We were both caught up in the illusion."

Twila's laughter was not pleasant to Renie's ears.

"He's an intelligent guy!" Twila howled. "How could he believe it?"

"Because he saw it. Men believe what they see. It would never on earth occur to him it could be a hoax. Besides, Dave has always believed in magical things. His books prove that."

"Oh, yeah, the books. Those goblins are scary, even to me."

"He didn't draw them."

"He thought them up. That's scary enough."

Renie sucked absently at the orange, knowing she needed the nourishment, but not wanting it. "I feel like an idiot getting myself into this situation, Twila. I couldn't bear it if Dave found out from somebody else. I'll talk to him today. Tell him about the movie and about the shoot this afternoon. Tell him I need to talk to him as soon as possible and ask him if I can meet him later today. Say around six. But just please don't tell him I'm a human being."

Eyes sparkling, Twila rose, looking at her watch. "Right. I'll not breathe a word about you being a human being."

Renie smiled up at her gratefully, still sucking at the orange. "Where is Tristan, by the way?"

"Fishing, I think. We're going to dinner tonight. You guys could join us if Dave is still speaking to you by then. Men hate to be made fools of, Auntie Ren."

"You keep saying that. I don't need to be reminded. The thing just got out of hand. I'll try to fix it."

DAVE WAS ON TIME at their usual meeting place, the marina entrance. He found Twila waiting. She waved him down and when he pulled to the curb, she said, "Renie can't make it until later. I want to talk to you, Dave. Will you buy me a beer?"

"Sure," he answered. "Get in."

He drove down the street to a small café.

When they were seated, drinks in front of them, Twila smiled and said, "The job Renie wanted came through. Well, we knew it would. The delay was just some contract stuff. So she's working already, and that's why she couldn't meet you." She paused.

Dave said nothing and waited for the rest.

"She's going to be in a movie," Twila said. "She's one of the stars. It's going to be shot right here on the coast, and she was asked not to say anything, because the studio wants to control all the advance publicity. And besides, they wanted to get set up before the local people got wind of it."

He was unable to hide his surprise. "Renie is an actress?"

Twila grinned. "She never has been an actress before, except for some college theater classes. This is her first real acting job. Actually, she doesn't have a lot of acting to do in this film. She plays a mermaid."

"A . . . mermaid," he repeated.

"Well, it . . . it's what she does best, after all. This is a film about a mermaid, so . . . so that's why she was asked to be in it."

"Asked by whom?"

"By the producer. He saw her at a collegiate swimming and diving competition a few years ago. Renie was in training for the Olympics, you know."

"I didn't know."

"Oh, yes. She was very good. Then she got badly hurt in a water-skiing accident and couldn't compete anymore. She's been coaching, but it's been a financial struggle for her until this film thing came along."

Dave frowned. "She was badly hurt?"

"Her back was hurt. She's worked like hell to regain her health."

"A film about a mermaid?" he asked, still confused.

"Uh . . . yes. They're taking some publicity pictures this afternoon. That's why she couldn't keep her date with you."

"Where are they taking these pictures?"

"Over in the unnamed cove. You know those tiny islands? They're going to shoot on one of those islands. And in the water as well."

So today, he thought, *she's a mermaid in the afternoon. Bloody strange, this.*

"I'm going over there," he said.

Twila blinked. "Over where?"

"The unnamed cove. I think I'd like to see this photocall. Do you want to come along?"

"Definitely." Twila smiled. "I need to get back to the Sandrine before too long, though."

"We'll drive. How close is the *Sandrine* to the north shore now?"

"Very close."

"Right, then. I'll pick up my rubber boat, so I can row you over from the shore, if you like." He finished his beer with one long, thirsty drink and waited for Twila to rise.

Twila took another sip and stood up. "Okay," she said gravely, as though there were some conspiracy in the making.

Walking to the car, he said, "It wouldn't do me any good to ask you about her, would it?"

"What do you mean?"

"I'm sure you know what I mean, Twila."

"Please don't put me on the spot, Dave. Auntie said she would meet you this afternoon around six. She said the two of you hadn't really had a chance to . . . talk."

He nodded. "For which I assume much of the blame."

Twila squeezed his hand affectionately. He wasn't sure what it meant, except that it was her way of saying she understood. What the devil it was she thought she understood, Dave didn't know. "All right, then," he conceded. "I won't ask you."

In truth, he thought, Twila probably wasn't the one to ask. He was beginning to have grave misgivings about Renie. He wanted to see her, and he wanted to see her now.

A mermaid film? Starring a . . . mermaid?

Or starring an Olympic hopeful who could swim like one? And who looked like one? God. Renie would have told him, wouldn't she?

Wouldn't she?

His head swam.

Half an hour later, he and Twila made their way along the rocky slope on the northern shore. They were only a few hundred meters from the cave where Renie had made love to him. The *Sandrine II* lay at anchor just off the ridge of darker water. The sea was the color of bright sapphires, reflecting the blue of the sky.

There was activity on the closest islet. A motor craft circled the lichen-draped rock with two photographers on board, one snapping pictures of the mermaid from every angle, the other wearing scuba gear. Renie had clearly not yet been in the water; her hair was dry and shining gold in the sunlight, brushed carefully over her breasts. Her tail sparkled like sequins. She held a comb in one hand and a mirror in the other, according to mermaid tradition.

Dave's heart pounded. He found no words as he lowered himself onto a smooth rock and motioned to Twila to sit beside him. It was like watching a performance in an amphitheater of sea and sky. A performance that infuriated him. He was consumed with seething jealousy.

Renie...the woman...he could share with the world, but the mermaid was different. Real or not, actress or not, the mermaid was his! She was his love—his memory...his secret.

She was a secret he did not want to share. And now, suddenly, without warning, she was no longer his. She belonged to all of them, to these men whose cameras preyed upon her and to the world that would see those pictures.

"She's beautiful," Twila said in a voice filled with awe.

"Dangerously so," he answered. His fists were tight.

The sun caught the reflection of the mermaid's mirror like a flash of fire.

They sat in silence for a very long time, watching Renie react to requests from the photographers, shifting her position and rearranging her glittering tail. Twila avoided looking at him. She said, "You're angry."

"Yes."

She sat very still, as if she dared not move. "You're very angry."

"Yes."

"Why? Because she didn't tell you?"

He didn't answer at once. "I suppose I have no right to be this angry. I don't own her."

The underwater photographer jumped into the sea, and a few seconds later Renie followed. She dived and circled, tail rising out of the water.

Dave wondered how she could do it. Remembering the weight of the tail when he'd carried her, he guessed the appendage must be lighter when buoyed by water. The scales had cut him. He'd had a very close look at those scales in the murky twilight, but had refrained from touching them, out of revulsion. Now he wished he had examined them more closely.

Twila said softly, "You're awfully quiet, my boy."

"I'm in a very bad mood."

The underwater session took less time than Dave had expected. Renie climbed back onto the islet with unneeded help from the diver, and posed for a few more shots with her hair wet and dripping and the water sparkling on her body.

The putt-putt of the motor broke the quiet peace of the golden-blue afternoon as the photographers pointed their boat toward the marina. Renie threw them the comb and mirror waved them off, and in only moments she was alone on the islet, shading her eyes, looking not toward the departing photographers, but in the opposite direction, toward the open sea.

"Row me home," Twila said. "I have to help her get aboard." She started to scurry down the rocks.

"I'll help her get aboard," Dave said, offering Twila his car keys. "You can drive back. Take your time. Do some shopping or something."

He stripped off his shirt and handed it to her. Then his shoes and socks and finally his jeans. Twila said nothing, only stood and smiled at him; her gaze ran up and down his body with admiration and not a shred of shame when he stood in his blue, French bikini briefs. He could still feel her eyes on him as he made his way down the slope and dived into the sea.

Renie did not appear to have seen them. Dave was well out into the waves when the mermaid slid off the slippery rocks and began swimming toward the yacht, a distance of only a few hundred meters.

He intercepted her halfway there.

"Dave!" she shouted. "I thought that must be you! What are you doing out here?"

"Looking for my mermaid!" he shouted back.

She did a little dive. He dived also, sweeping under her, awed by her grace in the water.

For a little while, he thought *she belonged only to me.*

They swam together, cavorting in the waves, gradually working their way to the boat. He watched her long hair sway in the water, saw her tail sparkle and the undulating motion of its gauzy fins. The graceful movements of her arms. Her firm, full breasts. But he could not see her eyes.

Dripping, Dave climbed up the chrome ladder off the stern and lowered the swing, leaning well over the railing to watch her pull herself on. She gave a hand signal and he cranked her up. She flopped onto the deck like a helpless, captured fish.

"Where is Twila?" she asked, out of breath.

"Driving my car in the general direction of Savenay." He stood over her, staring down.

Nervous, Renie glanced away, propping herself upon one elbow. "What did she tell you?"

"About the mermaid film. And the photographers."

She nodded. "And did you grill her about me?"

"She asked me not to."

Looking up at him, she squinted in the sun. "We need to talk."

"You know me. I'd rather make love than conversation."

He reached for the towels that were neatly stacked against the bulkhead and handed her one. With another he dried his face, then wrapped it around the fishtail to protect his skin, scooped her into his arms and carried her down the three steps from the deck, across the cabin to the captain's cabin in the bow, and laid her upon the bed.

He stepped out of his soaking-wet cotton briefs and without a word proceeded to dry her face and her body with gentle, sensuous strokes of the towel.

She asked, "Don't you want something...a towel to put on?"

"No."

"Dave, it's hard to talk to you when you're standing there naked. It interferes with my concentration."

"Concentrate just on me, then. I enjoy your concentration on me."

"No. This time I have to keep my head. There is something I must tell you."

"It can't be as important as this," he said, leaning over to kiss her shoulder.

"Will you stop that? You're playing a game."

"Who's playing a game?"

He moved his hands over her stomach and her abdomen to the top of the fishtail, carefully examining the scales with his fingertips, to avoid getting cut.

Renie fell into a deep silence, which told him that she knew what he was doing.

He manipulated his hand gingerly along the top of the appendage and across her abdomen to the curve of her pelvic bone. He pressed his fingers gently into the soft muscle and was able to get under the band.

Renie looked up at him and said nothing. He couldn't read what was in her eyes. She was neither smiling nor frowning. Obviously, she was waiting for a reaction.

There was none yet. Instead he explored further, circling his fingertips around her body until he came to a place where the hold began to give. Careful not to cut himself, he gave a slight tug and heard a gentle ripping sound.

"Velcro?"

She nodded.

He tugged harder, loosening the top enough to get his hand underneath. Beneath the tail was only her skin.

Dave drew back as the first rumbles began to form deep in his throat. Like bubbles rising in a beer glass, the rumbles rose and spilled out in a gale of uncontrolled laughter. He dropped beside her, leaning against the bulkhead for support and laughed until his eyes were moist.

Renie watched him until his laughter became infectious.

"Thank God you're laughing," she said.

"Thank God you're human!"

She breathed a giant sigh of relief. "I was afraid you were going to kill me."

"For what? For making a complete fool of me by letting me go on believing you were real...not real...half-real?"

"Yes. For that."

He continued to laugh. "I made a fool of myself. You didn't do it."

"I didn't stop you."

He touched her arm. "That first night I'm glad you didn't tell me. You let me have my illusion, and gave me magic I'll never forget. And yesterday when you tried to tell me, I wouldn't let you because I wanted to hold on to the magic. I feel like an absolute idiot, Renie. But God, it was fun!"

She smiled. "Yes! It was fun."

He kissed her forehead. "And you're human! How the hell could I be mad about *that*?"

"I never dreamed you'd be such a good sport."

"Sport? I fell under the spell of a siren. How many men can make such a claim? Then I discover the half woman I love is a whole woman. What did you think I'd do?"

"At worst, walk out of my life. At best, sulk."

"Babies sulk. Men don't sulk."

"Lesser men sulk," she insisted.

Still caught up in the joke on himself, he chuckled, buoyed by relief far greater than he could ever put into words. He asked, "How do we get you out of that thing?"

"Very carefully. It isn't easy. I can't do it alone." She found more seams of hidden Velcro and loosened them. "It can't be folded over. You have to pull it from the bottom and just ease it off, but slowly. Grab the very top of the my caudal fin . . . careful not to tear it."

"Don't worry. I've never torn a lady's caudal fin in my life."

Pulling steadily, he grunted, "It's like a snake shedding its skin. How the devil do you ever get into this?"

"Practice and powder."

When she had the use of her legs again, Renie rose from the bunk and stretched.

"Do you want me to do something with this carp suit?"

"Carp suit? I'm insulted."

"Don't be. I like carp. Goldfish are carp. They were my favorite fish until I met you. I had two goldfish as pets when I was a lad. Fugimaka and Malone."

She shook her head, smiling. "My goldfish was named Goldie. I had no imagination as a kid. Could you take the carp suit to the cockpit? I'm headed for the head for obvious reasons. I've been in that thing for hours."

Dave gathered the tail carefully, using the towel. "I have a lot to celebrate. Hell, *we* have a lot to celebrate! What do you have to drink?"

"Champagne," she answered. "Twila brought in a supply yesterday. It's on ice. You'll find a corkscrew on the countertop." She disappeared into the head.

When she came out, he had brought two glasses and a bubbling, open bottle into the captain's cabin. He was lounging on the wide berth, still naked, and held out his arms.

"Lie down here beside me, beautiful lady."

She snuggled next to him while he poured the champagne.

Holding up his glass to hers, Dave smiled. "Let's drink to illusions," he said. "No matter how real life gets, I'll always have my memories of a magical daughter of the deep who made me love again and gave me love in return."

Renie's eyes misted. "To illusions," she said.

He drained the glass quickly and poured another.

Renie dipped her fingers into her glass and touched his lips.

"Mmm," he murmured, licking the champagne from her fingertips. "Two can play this game...." He dipped his fingers and began circling her breasts sensually.

She watched him tip his glass and empty it over her.

"Oh, it's c—!" she started to protest, but fell silent when his tongue followed, tasting the champagne warmed by her body. She trembled in his arms.

"Did you ever bathe in champagne?" he asked, savoring the taste of her; salt from the sea, bubbling wine, the perfume of her skin.

"I have fantasized bathing in champagne."

"Then so shall it be, my lady."

He lowered her gently onto the berth, slid his arm free, held up the bottle and poured the frothy liquid through his open fingers, onto her body, all over her, watching the tiny bubbles rise and burst against her pale skin. "When I say I feel like celebrating, I mean I feel like *celebrating*...."

"It tickles...." Smiling, she closed her eyes, surrendering to the sensations.

He smoothed the spilled champagne in circular strokes over her thighs and torso and licked at it, grazing and tickling and fondling with his tongue, thirsting for love, grateful for love, grateful for her.

Her sighs were music.

The lapping of the waves against the hull was music.

Gently the ocean rocked them. The ocean would not take her away.

He made love to her softly, perfectly, and it seemed to him like the first time.

Without the helpless sadness of before.

11

THE FILMING was less grueling than Renie had feared it would be—she was not required to stay in the costume nor in the ocean for long periods. Two lighter, easier costumes were used sometimes, depending on the angles required for the scene of the moment. Only the motion picture's ocean scenes and some in boats were to be shot on location. The remainder of the film was to be completed in Southern California.

She did not see Dave the first day on her new job, but talked to him briefly and asked him to meet her at the end of the following day.

Renie didn't manage to get free until seven o'clock, half an hour late. Leaving the set, thinking about Dave, she didn't notice the reporters until they converged upon her. Blinding flashbulbs went off in her eyes. A video camera was pointed at her. Questions about the film and about herself were hurled at her like stones.

Taken by surprise, she looked from one reporter to the other, not knowing how to hurry this. Dave would not appreciate being kept waiting any longer. She tried to keep walking, tried to keep smiling and to answer the questions the best she knew how. Yes, it was her first film. Yes, she was from San Diego. No, she was not a close personal friend of Bryan Milstrom. . . .

Dave's car was parked at the curb just outside the wire fence. As she drew nearer, flanked by the reporters and cameras, the engine started and he pulled away without so much as a wave.

Stunned, Renie did her best to withstand the press assault with dignity, but had no way to escape, now that she could not duck into Dave's car as she hoped. Why would he deliberately leave her stranded like that?

Their questions seemed endless and pointless. Just outside the gate, a coffee stand had been set up by two men to whom Dave had introduced her in the bar at Cauvier, Edwin Noble, an Englishman who also lived in the village, and Émile, who spoke almost no English. Why these two had the concession and not someone else, she had no idea, but was glad she knew them. Right now the coffee stand gave her a destination.

Edwin Noble was still there, about to close up for the day. He must have seen her dilemma, for he was ready with a cup of coffee. He protested vigorously to the American reporters in French and pretended he could not understand their answers. While this was going on, Dave's small black car appeared again at the curb.

This time Twila was at the wheel. She left the engine running and bounced out, wearing a tight blue denim miniskirt, T-shirt trimmed in lace and earrings that hung to her shoulders. Smiling demurely at the reporters, she took her aunt by the arm and escorted her to the car, opening the door and gently pushing her inside. Renie tried to keep smiling; after all, the director had asked her to come across as sweet as possible in media encounters. The mermaid image: innocent and dangerous.

Twila jumped into the driver's seat and they sped away. Renie sputtered, "Where the hell is Dave? He was parked at the gate, waiting, and after I came out he just left me. Deserted me. That was less than fifteen minutes ago. How did you get his car?"

"Tristan and I were waiting at a café down the street for the two of you to meet us. Dave pulled right up to the door, all hot and bothered, ran in and asked me to pick you up.... Not Tristan. It had to be me. When I demanded to know why, he said he would explain later, but please just to do it because you were waiting. It was bizarre, Auntie Ren."

Renie bit her lip. "The photographers and reporters spooked him."

"He saw them?"

"Yes. Just before he booked it out of there."

"Whoa! The photographers, eh? Ye gods, he really *is* a jewel thief! Or even worse!"

"He's not a jewel thief."

"You don't think so? He doesn't act like an amnesiac, so what is he, then?"

"I don't know."

"He's hiding something," Twila said, gripping the steering wheel tightly. "A man who's not hiding something wouldn't have booked it like that. I heard he was a retired British secret agent who broke under enemy torture."

Renie stared at her. "You heard no such thing!"

"I swear I did. The Brit at the coffee stand knows him personally, so I was, you know, interrogating this guy

Edwin. He said he had heard the secret-agent story, but he wasn't sure if it was true, because Dave is pretty young to be retired unless the torture affected his mind."

"That village of Dave's must be a certified fable factory!" Renie wailed. "How do you manage to keep dredging up this stuff?"

"I'm looking for clues, and so should you be. I checked his fingernails. None of them are missing. I should have checked out his toenails when he took off his clothes to go swimming after you. But who could think of toenails at a time like that? What a body that guy has!"

"Will you stop? Dave told me himself that they tell stories about him in the village because he doesn't talk about himself."

Twila grinned. "Let's be honest. They tell stories about him because he is unforgivably good-looking—that's what triggers gossip. Women want him and men are jealous of him. Besides, since the beginning of time, villagers have been overcurious about mysterious, handsome strangers who suddenly appear in their midst."

"None of it explains his strange behavior tonight," Renie said, frowning. "There was a reason why he didn't want to be seen by those American reporters."

"I didn't realize they were American. So! The Americans have landed."

"The publicist announced the film yesterday. It didn't take them long to get here. Everybody wants to be first to find out who I am. I didn't anticipate this, Twila. It's going to take some getting used to."

"For your boyfriend, too."

"Yes. They kept asking if I had a boyfriend, as I was watching him disappear in a cloud of smoke. So I said no. I didn't dare sic them on Dave."

"He has some explaining to do," Twila said, turning onto the street where the café lay.

Inside, Tristan was smoking steadily. "We have reached a decision," he said, rising when the women walked up to the table. "We are all going up to Cauvier to dine at the restaurant in the village square."

Renie looked quizzically at Dave, who stood with glass in hand. He looked neither relaxed nor happy. Something was bothering him.

"I had no idea you were a celebrity," he said.

"Neither did I. It seems to have happened overnight."

"A lot of people like being in the circle of a celebrity," Twila commented, giving him an unfriendly stare.

Dave looked at her blankly, then shifted his gaze back to Renie. "Shall we go?"

He hadn't bothered apologizing for running off; in fact, he had barely greeted her. Dave and Tristan both seemed anxious to get out of the coast town and up the hill to the medieval village Dave called home. Renie had a feeling that whatever was bothering Dave was not going to be addressed until the two of them were alone.

Tristan had no car on the coast, so it was up to Dave to drive. En route he was quiet, but since he was never particularly extroverted in a group setting, this was not unusual. He reached over from the driver's seat, took her hand into his and squeezed affectionately.

In Cauvier, the four were walking through the village square when a young woman appeared around a corner and greeted Dave in French. She turned quickly to Renie and continued chattering in French. Neither Dave nor Tristan bothered to translate; it did not seem to concern either of them that Renie and Twila didn't know who the woman was and couldn't understand what she was saying.

Dave's first response was anger. A short, heated exchange followed, during which, at one point, Dave and Tristan exchanged fleeting, but very concerned, glances.

The Frenchwoman was definitely trying to get Renie's attention. When she addressed her for the second time, Renie signaled once again that she did not understand. After what sounded to her like more verbal sniping at Dave, the Frenchwoman turned and left, but not before offering Renie a soft word and a friendly smile.

"What on earth was that about?" she asked.

Dave rubbed his chin. In the light of the street lamp, his pale eyes were shining with frustration. "She's a reporter for the village weekly paper," he answered. "Word has spread about the filming going on, and she recognized you as the star of the picture. She wanted to interview you and send for a camera. I told her it was an invasion of your privacy and she would have to find you at the film set if she wanted to talk to you."

"*Mon Dieu*, you're famous," Tristan said, half under his breath.

"I wouldn't go so far as to use the word famous," Renie answered unhappily.

"Fame rapidly approacheth," Twila put in.

Renie sighed. From the little she had experienced so far, this wasn't going to be very pleasant. She was by nature a private person. Questions about the film were welcome enough. But questions about her personal life were another matter entirely. She had a lot to learn about handling this. Bryan had not sufficiently warned her.

"People are just curious about the film," she answered defensively, trying to make as little of it as possible.

That earlier glance exchanged between Tristan and Dave was bothering her. What the hell had it meant?

"Auntie Ren is too modest," Twila said. "There is a lot of publicity generating for this movie. She's on her way to fame and riches."

Dave scowled. "Let's skip the restaurant," he said. "Our Madame Rochet is the author of village gossip and determined enough to come back for another go, and with a camera next time. I suggest a full retreat. We can take cover at my fortress."

"Excellent," Tristan agreed, sliding an arm around Twila's waist.

Sure, Renie thought. *Let's run in full retreat the rest of the way up the hill.* She was feeling more uncomfortable by the minute.

THEY SAT on the garden terrace under the stars, drinking, while Morgan, just fed, slept under Dave's chair with a ball in his mouth. Tristan was telling Twila about his native Paris. Renie was barely listening. Dave was clearly not himself.

She had been closely watching Dave and Tristan all evening. By now she was convinced that Tristan knew about Dave's secret past. The knowing look between them, the fact that neither ever asked the other to explain anything that was said or implied. The fact that Tristan did not question Dave's paranoid reaction to cameras.

Tristan knew, all right. He knew which of Twila's yarns flirted with the truth. Dave trusted the mysterious Frenchman more than he trusted her.

If he loved her, as he said he did, then why hadn't he confided in her? Well, to be fair, there hadn't been a great deal of time. Perhaps he would confide in her tonight, if they had a chance to be alone, which was beginning to look doubtful.

Tristan seemed aware of the tenseness in the atmosphere. After the second drink, his limit apparently, he turned down Dave's halfhearted offer to cook omelets for dinner, saying that he and Twila would pop down to the village instead. The lovers wanted to be alone, he told Twila, and whisked her away in Dave's car, promising to return in time to get Renie back to the boat early. Twila had shifted into a maternal mode, insisting that Renie get a good night's sleep before tomorrow's filming.

When they were alone, Renie said, "I'm not hungry enough for an omelet."

"I'm not, either, to tell you the truth. Will bread and cheese and fruit do?"

"Fine. I don't want you to cook. I want you to talk. For someone who insists real men don't sulk, you've come dangerously close to contradicting yourself a couple times tonight."

"Not sulking in the true sense. I was deep in thought."

"I know."

"And I'm upset."

"Obviously."

She let him lead her through the garden door into the kitchen. He closed the door on Morgan and proceeded to wash some pears and peaches. He sliced bread and cheese and opened a bottle of wine, all of which he set up on the small kitchen table. His movements seemed automatic and his hands shook.

Neither of them sat down. Clumsily he poured the two glasses half-full and handed one to her. She took a small sip and set the stemmed glass upon the table.

"Talk to me, Dave. Tell me what's wrong."

He circled his arms around her and pulled her close. There were strain lines around his eyes, as if he were squinting. "I don't want to tell you, Renie. I have to, but I don't want to. All evening I've been trying to figure it out and I can't. Bloody hell, I just can't."

Renie knew by now that she didn't want to hear what he was going to say. They had to have this out, though; she couldn't stand it any longer. "You might as well just blurt it out, damn it! Does it have something to do with my being in the film?"

"Yes."

His hands felt cold on her arms, although the night air was warm. He was chilled from nerves. Frightened, she waited.

"It has nothing to do with how I feel about you," he began in a husky voice. "I love you, Renie. Please, never doubt that. I know you can't doubt that, after all we've been to each other. But I had no idea you were a film actress. No clue whatever about it...."

She saw he was having difficulty meeting her gaze. "And suddenly I'm exposed to publicity, interviews and cameras."

He closed his eyes, then opened them, and his eyes were dulled with pain. "I don't want to lose you, but I have to. And God knows, I didn't want to hurt you. Much as it kills me to say it, Renie, I can't..." His voice cracked. There was a white line around his lips. "I can't see you anymore."

Her heart stopped. A sharp pain pierced her like an arrow. She had feared it, feared he would say the worst. Renie stared at him, feeling tears begin to burn behind her eyes. Dreams were exploding in those forming tears . . . a thousand bright, soft dreams....

His voice rasped. "I'm sorry. I wish it didn't have to be like this, but it is. It just won't work for us."

Renie wanted to touch him, to hug him and squeeze away those awful words, make them go away, as if she had never heard them. She swallowed and said, "Just like that? I don't deserve the dignity of a logical explanation?"

"I have to get out of your life for your sake as much as for mine. Believe me. It's not choice. I have to."

Have to? How could he treat her like this? How could...? "This is just evasive double-talk, dancing all around the truth!" she blurted, hurt and angry. "What is it? Do you have a wife in England who might see photos of you, living it up on the Riviera with an American actress? That's it, isn't it?"

He stared at her with an expression she could not identify. Not exactly sadness, not exactly anger, not exactly confusion. She couldn't tell what it was, except that it frightened her.

"It's a...complicated situation," he hedged. His jaw was tight.

Her anger flashed hotter. "What else have you lied to me about?"

"It's more untruthful to say I have a wife than to say I haven't. Legally, perhaps. I don't know. My dilemma is very hard to explain."

"Then I suggest you try! I'm not an idiot, Dave. I'm not incapable of listening or of understanding. I know Tristan is privy to your secrets, anyone could tell that. You haven't been fair with me."

He rubbed his chin nervously. The look on his face was sad. No anger, no pleading for forgiveness. Only a sadness so deep that tears began to glisten in his eyes. His tears aroused such pain in Renie that she had to turn away.

"No, I haven't been fair," he said softly. "My only defense is that I believed you were...not a mortal woman, and therefore you could never truly be a part of my life. If I'd known the truth, I swear I would never have got involved with you. By the time I did know, I already loved you. I played a game with myself and convinced myself I could be with you, at least for a little while. Now you turn out to be not only a mortal but a celebrity. I can't...I can't manage that."

She pulled a chair from the table and sat down, forcing back the tears, stubbornly wishing to hide her pain. Renie felt her heart aching beyond endurance, but the reason for the pain . . . his pain . . . was so elusive. She had to know. He owed her that. He owed her the reason why. She tried to meet his eyes. "What are you running from? The law?"

"I'm not a criminal, if that's what you are asking."

"Why else would you be so camera shy?"

Dave sat down, too, and looked through the window at the lights of the garden, as if he could not stand her eyes on him any longer. His breathing was as fast and erratic as if he had been making love.

Curse remembering his love! Not now! Renie cried inside herself.

"Look," he began shakily. "I don't blame you for being furious, for feeling betrayed. I hate this. It's all my fault for trying to pretend, even for a few days, that I had a right to be with you. I dare tell you only this. . . . If you are with me, you will be in danger. I won't risk that, even if the cost is losing you. If anyone photographs us together, we could both be in danger."

His voice was hard when he spoke of danger, and this sent a shiver of fright through her. The danger he spoke of was close! She could feel it in the hardness of his words and in the shifting of his eyes. "In danger of *what?*" she demanded.

"I can't tell you that."

Her anger was turning to a pulsing, hot fear. Whatever the danger, it was part of his life. God, he had been living with his secret damn danger all the time she'd known him, while pretending to be a vagabond. That hadn't been totally convincing, she remembered. So he wasn't a carefree vagabond. She should have listened to her warning intuition.

Aware that anger was weakening her voice, she said, "You can't tell me what danger you're in, yet you say you're not a criminal? You're trying to scare me away. You don't have to try so hard, you know! I'm not going to hang on to you like a limp puppy if you don't want to see me anymore."

"I've hurt you," he said miserably.

"Of course you have. You meant to."

"I didn't want to." He drained the wineglass and leaned forward. His eyes had never been so pale. "Look, Renie. This thing is . . ." He poured the glass full and drank several swallows more. "In England I witnessed a heinous crime. For reasons I can't explain, I couldn't come forward. I've put my life in jeopardy because of it. I'm sorry for talking in riddles, but I can't do otherwise without endangering you. Please don't ask me any more questions. I don't want you to know any more or be involved with me any further. I can't bear responsibility for anything happening to you. I'd prefer to have you hate me."

She felt the world closing in around her. "If you are innocent, why can't you go to the police?"

"Because I'm a suspect."

She gasped. "Then you *are* a fugitive!"

"By definition, yes. Now please stop—"

"Tristan knows. Doesn't he?"

He nodded. "Tristan is trying to get me out of this mess. Now stop asking me, Renie. All I can do is hope you believe I love you. I wish things were different."

She buried her face in her hands. *Don't cry!* she told herself. It seemed very important that Dave should not see her cry, even if tears sparkled in his own eyes when he tried to look at her. "Well," she mumbled into her hands. "I guess that's it, then."

"I beg you not to talk to anyone about me," he said. "I know you don't owe me anything, but this I beg of you."

"You are in grave trouble, aren't you?"

"Yes."

Her heart went out to him. To the pain he was suffering that caused his hands to tremble and tears to moisten his eyes. The pain of loving her and having to let her go. Perhaps he really was a criminal, she thought, crushed by his rejection. What if he was making up the part about being witness to a crime, and he himself had committed the crime, as the police evidently believed? No. If that were so, he would have chosen to make up some fake, logical story that explained everything neatly and tidily. He could have, but he hadn't.

Renie felt dizzy. Her head spun crazily. This man she loved—the police were after him. And maybe someone else. *Why?*

"If you trusted me," she said, "You'd confide in me."

"It's not a matter of trust, it's a matter of love."

"You should have told me before I . . ." *Before I loved you,* she wanted to say, but didn't.

"I thought the dangers of this world could not touch you. I thought you belonged to the sea." His lips quivered with the emotion he could no longer restrain. "Or maybe I just wanted to believe it, because I needed to love again. And I had met you."

Unable to bear looking at the pain in his eyes, she rose from the table. "I'm going back out into the garden. I'm not able to deal with all this. I don't think I can ever deal with this."

To her surprise, he disappeared suddenly with no explanation and left her standing alone in the doorway. Alone...without him. She pushed open the heavy wooden door and stepped into the evening cool, not feeling the soft ocean breeze, not smelling the perfume of the flowers, not aware of anything but pain. The tears came and spilled down her face. She ached all over. Her impulse was to run, but there was nowhere to go, except into the darkness.

Dave came up behind her as she gazed at the distant view of the unnamed cove and stood at her side. His nearness was like a warm wave in a cold sea. She had allowed herself to think he would always be there to warm her. Now he was gone, but not quite. She reeled at his nearness.

"I won't say anything," she said softly. "I won't tell anyone about you. I'll try to forget I ever knew you."

"I won't forget you, Renie. Our time together has meant more to me than you'll ever know. Someday, somewhere, I'll try to get up the courage to go see your film. I might die from the pain of seeing my illusion come to life again before my eyes, but I won't be able to stay away from the theater. I will never...never forget you...."

In her hand he placed a small, carved statue of a dove.

Renie gazed at it through her tears.

"I've had it with me for years," he said. "To bring me luck. It brought me you. Take it as a remembrance of my love, and know that my love for you will last until this little bird can fly." His hands trembled in hers. "Know that I loved you enough to leave you...."

Loved you enough to leave you.... In the dark of the garden, Renie was able to hear what he was begging her to hear; he would not bring danger to her because he loved her.

She reached up to him and kissed his eyelids gently. Clutching the dove—his farewell gift—she returned to him the treasured words from her memory of days—a lifetime—ago. "It might as well be made of gold. The memories of you...have made me rich."

He closed his eyes, groaning softly, and took her into his arms. For the last time.

They stood in agonized silence, for there was nothing more to say. From the distance came the sound of a car. Tristan had known he shouldn't be away very long, she thought; he had known Dave was going to leave her tonight.

Dave moved his lips over her moist cheek and mouth and kissed her deeply. She tasted the salt of tears in his kiss. He said nothing more and neither did she. She pulled out of his embrace, clutching his strange charm of good luck, and turned, to walk out of the garden and out of his life.

Not knowing why.

MORGAN, only rarely concerned with the emotions of human beings, unless those emotions directly affected him, was subdued as he followed his master into the house.

He reminded Dave that food was still on the table and led the way to it. Still numb, Dave followed. He gave the dog a chunk of the cheese and went to his study with the remainder of the wine. On top of a stack of papers on his desk was his amateur sketch of the mermaid.

Mermaids disappear. They always do....

He should have known he couldn't keep her. Clenching his fists, he fought down the hurt, pushing it far inside, intending to leave it there and not let it out anymore. The pain would be a part of him, like his heart and lungs were parts of him. He would have to live with it.

It would not do to fantasize about being free someday to come back to her.... A man does not ask a woman to wait indefinitely for a lover who may never come. Hell, a mermaid was one thing. A woman was another. He dare not let a woman get too close to him, certainly not a woman he loved.

Anger wrapped itself around his deeper agony. One hasty, impulsive decision two years ago had got him into this mess. He glanced at the drawings of Fireskog, the hairy goblin, the memory assailed him, and that alone was enough to make his stomach start hurting again.

Unnoticed, I back out of the jetway and return to the terminal, swallow a handful of pills and drop onto a chair, waiting for the worst of the pain to subside. When it does, after the doors to my flight have closed, I find the nearest men's room.

The swarthy-faced man with two fingers missing on his right hand is in the men's room. He has not boarded the flight, either. I notice because the man's ticket and boarding pass are clearly visible, lying on top of his briefcase. Feeling ill, I think little of it now, in the men's room. Washing the perspiration from my face, I catch the image of the second man in the mirror—the individual who had walked into the lounge and made eye contact with the first, and then walked away.

Weak and dizzy, I walk into the main terminal, where I buy tea and sit for a time in the tea room. Still in pain, I don't feel up to standing in a line to turn in my ticket. The ticket matter can be done later. Anytime later.

Anytime later, he thought as he sat in lonely misery after two years on the coast of southern France. There had been no "later."

Dave's shoulders hunched over the desk, he stared at the drawings in front of him and sipped at the wine to try to dull the pain.

There had been no "later."

In a taxi, heading from Heathrow into London, I sit with my head back, holding my stomach. The taxi driver begins babbling excitedly about a plane going down, and turns up the radio. Minutes after takeoff a plane has exploded over the sea. The number of the flight is the one I should have been on. I am stunned. According to the report, there are no survivors.

Shocked into silence, I begin to tremble. My name will be among those listed as dead.

Sitting in the cab, I imagine being dead.

Just . . . dead. No more worries about the failure of my business. No more confrontations with Sarah.

Suppose I never surfaced, but remained dead? There would be no insurance fraud because I had no life insurance. Sarah would inherit my shares of the business, our personal bank accounts and investments, the house and everything in it. Even the dog. And myself?

I am carrying the £ 380,000 in cash to buy a shipment of art from the tribal artisans themselves in Zimbabwe, Zambia and Malawi.

The situation I find myself in is mind-boggling. Through some strange twist of fate—that pain in my gut—I'm alive.

I have taken life too much for granted, squandered and wasted years, living from day to day in the prison of routine and dead emotions. I am alive, but my life is a sham.

I have the chance to start over again . . . start to live again. A tempting thought. I even know where I can obtain documents for a false identity.

By the time I reach London, I have made the decision. I ask to be let out on an unfamiliar street corner. Already I am thinking of Cauvier, the small village in the sun that I discovered once, years ago, on holiday.

"What an idiot I was," Dave said to the bull terrier. "I couldn't even speak French." The dog cocked his head sympathetically. Dave shook his head in self-contempt. "I couldn't understand the news broadcasts, couldn't read a newspaper. All I could think that first fortnight was getting treatment for my ulcer, finding this house with the sea view, and trying to learn enough French to communicate." Dave chewed on a piece of bread and repeated, "What an idiot I was, Morgan! Now look at the mess I'm in."

He gazed with affection at the dog. "If they get me, Morg, you'll be back on your own again."

Eventually I learn that a bomb exploded on board the plane. Slowly, and with horror it begins to dawn on me that if anyone were to learn I am alive, I would be such a hot suspect in the bombing that I might never convince authorities I am innocent. I have all that cash. I have personal reasons to fake my own death. I have planned my escape with fake identification. Changed my name.

A bad mistake, that impulsive decision. I look guilty as hell, especially if there are no other leads.

I have not planned an exile as dangerous or as final as this.

Too late I remember the two characters who had been in the boarding lounge and later in the men's room. Thinking back, I am certain they are involved because their behavior was so suspicious. Like me, at least one of them had a ticket but never got on the plane. I alone can identify them and place them at the boarding gate. But to try it is to put myself among the accused. I'm the one who has taken a false name and fled. They will nail me.

My conscience won't let me rest. My only way out of this dilemma is to get the terrorists arrested, something I can help with and don't dare, in case it doesn't work. In the slight possibility I'm wrong, I could be asking for a death sentence.

Finding Tristan is a stroke of luck. If his group can track the terrorists, I can come out of hiding to identify them. But not before.

He was drinking steadily. The dog's eyes were riveted on him. "Forget it, Morg. Wine makes you sick."

He sat back, pushing aside the drawing of the mermaid; it made him sad. He had lost Renie because of his damned secrets. Now the loneliness was more than he could bear.

"Renie is right, Morg! She said if I loved her, I would tell her the truth. Curse it all, she's right!"

But Dave was afraid for her. If the terrorists found out he was alive, they might go after Renie to get to him. Who could predict what they would do? They had already killed three hundred people. Not one photograph of Renie must ever be taken with him. No one must ever associate the two of them.

"Bloody hell, Morgan. What a mess I've made of everything!"

12

TWILA ANGRILY TOSSED a yellow canvas cushion across the cabin of the *Sandrine II*. "Englishmen! All suave and mannerly on the exterior and all the while weaving webs of lies like spiders!"

Renie sighed. "And Frenchmen? I have a feeling you shouldn't get too involved with Tristan Escoiffier, either. I don't know what those two guys are up to. Promise me you'll be careful, Twila."

"I'm always careful."

"You're never careful. You don't know the meaning of the word—and you don't know anything about this man except that he's a friend of Dave's. And that isn't a very good recommendation."

"I realize that. I hate Dave Andrews for finking out on you. How come you have such monstrously bad luck with men, Auntie Ren? Why do you always fall in love with such devious men?"

"Always? I don't think I do. I've never been in love before. Not like this. This is the real thing. I wish you wouldn't rub it in, Twila. I'm hurting like hell right now."

"I could kill him. Is this fiasco going to interfere with your work?"

"Of course not." Renie, picking up her sweater from the bench, found the four Wizard's Fireside books underneath it. She'd have to return the books; they'd been the only copies on his shelf. She sat down and leafed through the colorful books for the dozenth time. The man who wrote these stories was the Dave Andrews she wanted to know and couldn't.

"You ought to get to bed," Twila was saying. "I prescribe two aspirins dissolved in brandy for a good night's sleep. Remember you're becoming a bright and shining star of the wide screen. Soon ten thousand men will want you."

"And I want only one." Twila had guessed right about the headache. Renie hadn't expected Dave to leave her, to say goodbye forever. She hadn't been prepared for the pain.

It was no consolation at all to know that he was hurting, too.

The ship's phone buzzed.

"It's him, wanting you back!" Twila exclaimed.

"No, I don't think so. It might be something about tomorrow's schedule." She picked up the phone.

"*Bonsoir*, Renie. It's Tristan here. Might I speak with Twila?"

"Of course." She handed over the phone and listened to one side of the conversation.

Twila's smile quickly vanished. "Do you know when you'll be coming back? . . . Yes . . . Thanks, Tristan . . . Yes, it has been. . . . You, too. . . . Sure, if you do. . . . *Au revoir*." She put the phone down slowly, with a scowl. "That slime!"

"He's leaving?" Renie asked.

"He said he called his home office after he got home tonight and there was a message for him. Urgent business. He's going back to Paris. Interesting coincidence, don't you think?"

"Did he leave a way for you to reach him?"

"Nope. Said he hopes to get back to the coast while we are still here, but he isn't sure." Twila grabbed the cushion and tossed it again. "Liar. He probably has a wife in Paris. A wife and six bratty kids."

Renie picked up the cushion. "You're not emotionally involved with Tristan. I know you, and I can tell you're not."

"No, thank God. And maybe he really was called away by his work, whatever the hell that is. But then again, maybe he wasn't. Do you think this has something to do with Dave and you breaking up?"

"It's hard to say. We have no way of knowing, and I don't think it would do any good to ask Dave."

Twila went to the galley and took a brandy bottle from the cabinet. "Well, the hell with them."

"I want only a sip of that," Renie said. "And then I'm going to try to get some sleep."

How long would Dave and she have lasted, she wondered, *had it not been for the cameras?*

The sea, at least, was friendly, and rocked the boat like a cradle as she lay on the berth where Dave had made love to her. Renie needed its comfort. The motion of the sea held her like an old friend, who would always be there for her.

DAVE WAS LEARNING more than he ever wanted to know about being a fugitive from his own past. One way or another, he thought, he was going to have to get control of his life. He was sick to death of running.

Tristan had left very suddenly. Whether or not he knew which project had caused him to be called away was unclear. But his departure made Dave uneasy.

For the next two nights he worked through the midnight hours until the words on his computer screen were blurring. He slept until nearly noon. He was trying to bring the story of the mermaid Silka to a close, but it was difficult to leave her.

Renie had paid a high price for loving him.

His creative energy flowed from the emotions that were choking him. *What good was freedom, if it came with the death of trust?*

In the late morning on the second day after he'd said goodbye to Renie, Dave was brushing his teeth when the telephone rang. He wiped his mouth hurriedly and caught the phone on the third ring.

"I have to make this short," Tristan said in English. "You have to make a move. Get a plane to London and turn yourself in."

"What?" Dave's brain reeled. It was the first time Tristan had phoned his home. Only urgency would prompt it. "Does this mean you've made arrests?"

"No. It means you've been seen and identified. This investigation has involved hundreds of people. I can't be sure who saw you because I don't have access to police records, but my spies assure me your identity is no longer a secret, so your arrest must be close. That, however, Davey, is not what concerns me. If the police know, probably so does the terrorist organization."

Tristan was not prone to panic, but there was urgency in his every word. "Get yourself to London fast, *mon ami*, before they find you, and hope the British police do not intercept you on the way. It would not look good."

Dave felt the muscles tense into knots across his shoulders. "Where are you?"

"I am on my way to London. I'll see you there. Now I must go. And so must you, quickly. Today, my friend."

Dave hung up the phone; his head was throbbing. He made his way down the stairs, Morgan at his heels, let the dog into the garden and put on a kettle of water for tea. *So this is it,* he thought. He was heading for prison for as long as it took the law—or Tristan's group—to find those men.

Once more he was going to disappear. This time leaving behind the woman he loved.

It wasn't fair to Renie. He couldn't just go without a word, without any explanation. Dave held his aching head. His game with the law was just about over; he might as well tell her now. The only kind thing to do was to talk to her before he left and explain what she had begged him to explain two days ago. Now that he had been located, there was no need for the masquerade.

Maybe, just maybe, she would someday understand. Maybe there was a chance for them in the future, when the terrorists were behind bars and this mess was over. Perhaps she might eventually forgive him.

At least, after today he wouldn't be running anymore, once he reached London. Being a fugitive was destroying him; it had cost him everything—his future, as well as his past.

He would leave Cauvier early this evening and get the first flight out of Nice in the morning. That left him only half the day to get organized and find a way to talk to Renie; it was already afternoon.

AN HOUR AN A HALF LATER, after he had posted his latest manuscript to England, Dave entered the bar in the village square, glad to find Edwin Noble at his usual table.

"We've missed you for a few days," Edwin said in greeting. "Have you deserted us for the lovely American mermaid?"

Dave sat down and waved at Victor, who knew what he wanted to drink. "What is this I hear about you and Émile setting up a coffee stall at the film set?"

"Entrepreneurs, aren't we? It was my idea, and Émile's brother had the right connections in Savenay. We're doing stunningly well. Americans consume an enormous quantity of coffee. The trick is, you see, to make the coffee sickeningly weak and liters of it. I see Mademoiselle Renie every day. Charming lass, truly charming. You're a lucky man, mate."

Dave's *pastis* was set in front of him. He drank it thirstily. "Where is Émile?"

"At the set. We take turns."

"What time does the filming usually stop for the day?"

Edwin absently shuffled a deck of cards. "The last two days they've finished around five."

"I want to meet Renie this afternoon. I need to talk to her. Does she leave about then?"

The other man nodded. "And she always stops to say hello."

"Good," Dave said. "If for any reason she gets out early, will you ask her to wait for me? Tell her it's important. It's impossible to contact her while she's working."

"Of course." Noble looked up from the deck of cards. "Is something bothering you, mate? You seem anxious and out of sorts."

Dave took another drink. "Something has come up. I have to leave today, Edwin. For London. I don't know when I'll be able to get back. It could be weeks, possibly months."

"Bloody hell. This is sudden."

"Yes." Dave sat forward and lowered his voice. "Look, Edwin. What I'd like to do is leave the keys to my house and my car with you. Please use the car all you like. The house, too, for that matter. Could you look after Morgan until I get back?"

Edwin gazed at him curiously for some time, then nodded thoughtfully. "Morgan is fond of me. After all, I've known him since before you came—in fact, since he was abandoned in the square." He shook his head and pulled a face. "Yes, I'll look after Morgan. Morgan and I are fast friends."

"You're a good fellow," Dave said gratefully. Unspoken, but doubtless heard by Edwin, was Dave's gratitude for his countryman's refraining from asking questions. Edwin Noble himself had a past he talked little about. Both expatriates lived only in the present.

"I take it you're leaving this evening, then, after you talk to Renie. I'll drive you to the Nice airport."

"Thanks," Dave said.

"It's the least I can do, since you're leaving your car with me."

Finishing the drink, Dave forced a smile. "You'll be down in Savenay, then, closing up your coffee business for the day. I'll meet you there around six."

"Right." Edwin Noble looked at his watch. "It's time I got down there, as a matter of fact, to relieve Émile." He grinned. "The timing with the car is lucky for me because my old van is due for some major repairs. These days, I'm surprised every time the engine agrees to start."

The two men walked together out of the smoky bar into the sunlight of the village square. A nagging sadness filled Dave, a phase of his life was over. The future was hard to predict, but he knew that on his return—whenever that might be—everything would be different. He would no longer be a fugitive or a victim of his own ill-reasoned destiny. However long it took, the next time he walked in the sun of this village square, he would be a free man.

But by that time Renie would be half a world away, immersed in her own life and lost to him.

RENIE LOOKED AT HER WATCH as she walked from the building, carrying a heavy bag with a thick script, the books she had borrowed from Dave and a change of clothes. Four-twenty. Twila was to meet her around five o'clock. Luckily there were no waiting reporters. Many had already left with their interviews of the director and herself. They would be back, though, because in three days' time, her costar, Steve Stevenson, was due to arrive.

Renie walked to the concession stand. Traffic on the street was heavier than usual and noisy. Edwin Noble met her with a smile and a steaming cup of coffee.

"You're a saint," she said, setting the heavy bag on the ground in front of the stand.

"Did it go well today?" he asked.

"Great. What is amazing to me is how they shoot all these scenes and camera angles that have nothing to do with the sequence of the film. The sequences are all put together later. Everything has to be so incredibly organized. They tell me exactly what they want me to do and I do it. It's quite fun, it really is." She blew on the coffee and took a sip. "You haven't seen Twila around here, have you?"

"No. Do you expect her?"

"Yes. We're going to do a little shopping and have dinner out."

"Dave should be here, too," Edwin said. "He wants to meet you here."

Her heart pounded a little faster. "When did he say this?"

"A couple of hours ago. He has something important to talk to you about."

She gazed quizzically at the Englishman. "You sound as though you know what it is."

"In part, yes. But he must be the one to tell you."

Renie set down the cup. "Oh, come on, Edwin. What's going on?"

Edwin stopped to serve coffee to some other customers. Renie waited impatiently. When they had gone on their way, she tried again. "You said important. Is it really important, Edwin?"

"Aye. The lad is leaving the coast, it seems. For an unspecified time."

Renie blinked back hot tears that had suddenly formed behind her eyes. He had already left her life; why did news of his leaving the coast envelop her in such complete, black emptiness? It was the finality of it! The goodbye forever. Forever.... "Leaving? Why?" she asked, fighting for control of her voice.

"He will have to tell you that. The truth is, I don't know myself." Edwin looked at his watch and checked the huge, gurgling percolator. The blue-and-white-striped awning above their heads flapped in the breeze, making popping sounds.

Renie turned and scanned the street. A moment or two later she saw Dave approaching on foot, wearing jeans and sneakers and a gray sweatshirt, his dark hair blowing softly over his forehead, looking more handsome than she had ever seen him. *This is how I'm going to remember him*, she thought, her heart aching so hard, she felt the physical pain. *This will be the last time I ever see him.*

To think that he was coming only to say a final goodbye was more pain than she had ever bargained for or prepared for. It might have been easier to have let it go with that sweet kiss in the garden.

She set the cup upon on the counter, and was reaching to pick up her bag when she saw two men in business suits flank him on each side. Dave was obviously startled to see them. He ducked back, as if to avoid them, but they closed in.

Trouble. It happened very quickly. Dave took a swing at one, hitting him so hard on the jaw that he tripped and fell backward. The second man punched Dave in the stomach.

"Edwin!" Renie shrieked. "Who are those men?"

"I have no idea," he answered, leaning over the high counter to get a better view. "I've never seen either of them."

The fight worsened as Dave punched back and was punched again. They were big men, but for a time he managed to hold his own against the two of them. A crowd began to gather.

Watching in horror, Renie instinctively stayed back. Dave's face was cut and bleeding, another man's nose was bloodied. Taking a kick to his groin, Dave doubled over. One of the men was able to force a handcuff onto his wrist. By this time the police had arrived.

Shouting and waving his arms, a young gendarme pushed back the crowd and there was an animated conversation in French. Both the men Dave had been fighting pulled out identification, which the policeman examined closely.

Dave struggled against the restraints and protested vehemently in French, with groans of pain between his words.

Renie gasped. "What is he saying, Edwin? Can you hear what he's saying?"

"No, I can't hear over the noise of the crowd. People are mumbling something about Italian secret police, but those blokes don't look like Italians to me. Bloody hell, they must be some kind of police, though, Renie."

"I don't believe this, Edwin!"

Handcuffed, still struggling, Dave was led away by the dark-suited men, one on each side. The local police officer was attempting to keep back the crowd. When they passed her, Dave looked up and their eyes met instantly. Renie realized he had been aware all along that she was there.

She rushed forward and started to say his name, but his eyes stopped her—his eyes and an almost imperceptible shake of his head. Unmistakably he was asking her . . . warning her . . . not to approach him, not to identify herself with him.

Renie stopped short. Dave turned away and did not look back again. Because his hands were cuffed, he was unable to wipe away the blood that was running down his face from a cut near his temple. The fact that he was in pain showed in his walk. He was still struggling, muttering to his captors in low tones.

They forced him to a halt at a parked car not far from the gate. Renie raced forward, to get as close as possible, not caring that tears were streaming down her cheeks. The pain in her chest was like a vise, almost strangling her.

Less than four meters away now, she stood in the pushing crowd and watched helplessly while one of the men shoved Dave roughly into the back seat of the car and climbed in after him. As the second man stood holding the door, ready to close it, Renie gasped and nearly cried out.

The man had two fingers missing from his right hand.

Like the goblin Fireskog!

My God! she thought. *Dave knows these guys! These men are not police! They are the danger Dave tried to warn me about!*

Her mind whirled. Dave had said he'd witnessed a crime. It had to be true! Now that she thought about it, he had written the whole account in the Wizard's Tales!

The Wandering Prince of Lost Clouds was Dave; she had sensed that all along. And the villains—the evil goblins Fireskog and Grig—were actual people, too! The three-fingered right hand of Dave's captor proved it. *He knew this man!*

Renie wanted to scream.

She grabbed the sleeve of the French policeman and did scream. In English. "You don't know who these men are! These are not police! Don't let them take him!"

The gendarme looked at her blankly, shook his head in anger and tried to push her back with the rest of the small crowd.

She was ready to pounce on the three-fingered man when she heard her name called, loudly and shrilly. Twila was racing to her side. The three-fingered man smiled reassuringly at the local police officer, walked around the car and got into the driver's seat.

Renie whirled around. "Twila! Where's your taxi?"

"Right behind me with the engine running. I was just—"

"Come on!" She pushed through the crowd, struggling with her heavy bag, not caring how many people she smacked into, trying to get to the curb.

"Hurry up, Twila!"

Twila slid into the back seat of the taxi, right behind her. "Renie, what the hell is—?"

"Follow that car!" Renie shouted to the driver, pointing in the direction of the gray sedan that had just pulled out, a few cars ahead of them.

The driver turned and looked at her as if she were crazy.

"Twila, you've been doing this cab thing! Tell him to follow that car and not to lose it!"

It was unnecessary. The taxi driver grinned, pointed to the car in question and shrugged elaborately. *"Oui, mademoiselle!"* Without so much as a glance fore or aft, he roared into the traffic. Brakes squealed behind them.

"What's going on?" Twila demanded. "What was all the yelling and crowding on the sidewalk?"

Renie was on the edge of the seat, her eyes pinned on the car they were following. "You didn't see?"

"No, I just drove up. What was it?"

"Dave. Two men came after him on the street and they had a horrible fistfight, and then these two thugs handcuffed him and threw him into that car and a policeman let it happen! They had some kind of false ID and pretended to be arresting him! They've kidnapped him!"

"Hold on! You lost me back there, Auntie Ren!"

"I think they intend to kill him!"

"What? You mean he really *is* a secret agent?"

"No. It's—" She stopped as the taxi screeched around a corner, knocking her into Twila's lap.

Both women sat forward again, their heads nearly in the front seat. Only one car was between them and the gray sedan now. The driver, enjoying himself, was grinning and honking his horn at every car on the street.

"It looks like they're turning into the marina!" Twila exclaimed.

"They are!"

The sedan slowed, pulled into the main gateway and proceeded to a parking area that was designated for marina clients only. Renie fumbled in her purse for money, with hands shaking so hard she could barely manage to find the bills she was after. The taxi driver pulled to a stop after the sedan parked.

"We'll get out here," Renie said, handing him a wad of bills. *"Merci!"*

He gave them a thumbs-up with a smile as they ducked into the shadows of a building; from there they could see the two men in suits get out of the other car and roughly pull Dave after them.

Twila kept muttering obscene phrases of disbelief. "Who are they, Auntie Ren?"

"Goblins," she whispered, her voice breaking with emotion. "The goblins in the Wizard's Tale! I don't know who they are, except that they are Dave's enemies."

"How do you know that?"

"The books," she answered impatiently, while they watched the three proceed along one of the piers. "The three-fingered goblin in the books. One of those men has only three fingers on his right hand!"

"I don't get it!"

"I don't either, exactly. But I know those are not law-enforcement people. I'd bet my life on it. They're taking him to a boat, Twila! What are we going to do?"

"We?"

"They'll kill him if we don't do something!"

"They'll kill us, too, if they're that determined. There's nothing we can do, except go to the police."

In silence they watched the three men move down the pier, onto a catwalk, and board one of the docked motor cruisers, a rusty, slow one, used mostly by local fishermen and scuba divers.

"Are you going to tell me what you've been sputtering about?" Twila whispered fiercely.

"Dave told me he had witnessed a crime and the people who did it might be after him. I'm sure that's who these men are."

Twila's eyebrows shot up. "Are they murderers?"

"I don't know. I think they might be."

"Omigod! What if the boat leaves?"

Renie's heart was pounding in her throat. "We'd better get to the police station, fast. Do you know where it is?"

"Only half a block from here. I've seen the police cars outside. It's that tiny white building with a flag."

They moved back, staying in the shadows of the trees. The sense of urgency was foremost in her mind. They must be planning to take Dave somewhere by sea. If he was the only witness to a crime they had committed, there was little question what his fate would be.

Hurrying down the street, which followed the curve of the beach, Twila panted, "What if you're wrong, Auntie Ren? What if these really are police?"

"I know I'm not wrong because Dave knew them. And I doubt he would have fought the police."

"That depends on what he did," Twila concluded doubtfully.

Breathing hard, they entered the police station. Renie rushed up to the low table at which two men in uniform sat. "There has been a kidnapping!" she said. *"Parlez-vous anglais?"*

The men shook their heads. Renie turned, to see the young gendarme who had been at the fight scene enter the building. He gave her an unfriendly look and said something in French, after which a man in civilian clothes appeared from an archway and came forward, saying haltingly, "I speak a very little English. What is wrong here?"

"Villains," Renie said carefully. "Criminals. They have kidnapped my friend. They took him to the marina . . . to a boat. They will kill him. You have to do something!"

Words and glances were exchanged by the Frenchmen. The one with the little English spoke vigorously to the officer who'd been a witness at the scene. Then he turned back to Renie. "These men were law enforcement," he said carefully.

"No, they weren't . . . were not!"

He walked to a side desk and produced a fax printed in French. Dave's photo was on it. The rest of the page needed no interpretation.

"I don't care what this says! These guys were not law enforcement!"

The man smiled patronizingly. "What evidence for this accusation?"

"Go on, tell him," Twila challenged. "Tell him about the three-fingered goblin."

Renie looked at her desperately. "He knew one of the men," she said. "He knew the one with only three fingers on his right hand." She held up three fingers. To Twila, she said, "The books. I have the books in my bag." She reached down and pulled one out.

"I don't know if that's such a great idea, Auntie Ren!"

"I'm desperate, Twila. These are intelligent men. I'll simply explain that as an author...he identified the criminals."

She held open the book in front of the policeman who spoke English and pointed to the hairy Fireskog with his three-fingered hand. "Here. You see? This is proof he knew him. He *wrote* about these men in this book!"

The gendarme gazed at the picture. He showed it to another and they both gazed at it. The goblin had a fierce growl and was throwing stones at the fat Fir Bolg Soldier.

"The hand," Twila said, pointing, trying to be helpful.

The other two men walked up for a look at the picture, too. One of them turned a page. On the next page Fireskog was tromping through the night fires of the Will-o'-the-Wisp, trying to frighten the Light Fairies from their homes under the toadstools.

Twila and Renie looked at each other.

The men in the police station looked at each other. One of them handed the book back to Renie very gently.

"Surely, *mademoiselle*, this is a little joke," the one who spoke English said at last, clearly trying very hard to be polite and not make eye contact with his fellow gendarmes. His eyes were dancing.

"Do we look like we're joking?" Twila yelled.

It was obvious to Renie that the men were calling upon every self-restraint they'd been taught in police training to keep from laughing in her face. "It's no use, Twila. They don't believe us. Dave is in the gravest danger and they don't believe us."

"They've taken this man to a boat!" she said to the policemen in desperation. "Will you just check it out? Make a phone call to...to London or wherever this fax came from? Won't you do *something*?"

"Of course, *mademoiselle*. We will check."

Renie turned. "Let's go. Let's get out of here."

In the street, Twila said, "They're not going to do anything. They think we're nuts! Why did you have to drag out that stupid book?"

"I guess it wasn't the most brilliant thing to do. But they asked for evidence. Damn it, Twila, I can't think straight. They're going to kill Dave! I know they are!" Her hands were shaking from the fear and frustration, and her eyes filled again with tears.

Twila squeezed her hand. At a fast, frantic pace, they were half running, half walking toward the marina. From the wide sidewalk they had a clear view of the rows of boats and the ocean beyond. From the entrance they could see someone on the deck of the boat where Dave had been taken and another man on the catwalk.

"They're pulling in the lines!" Twila cried. "They're going to leave!"

Horrified, tears streaming down her face, Renie grasped Twila's arm. "Where would they go? They must be meeting someone at one of the yacht basins up the coast."

"Probably," Twila agreed. "They could hardly use an airline, could they?"

The old boat cruised slowly through the harbor channel and past the orange buoys at the mouth.

"They're turning north!" Renie exclaimed.

"Yeah, up the coast, like you said." Twila's voice was husky. "Why won't anyone listen to us? I feel so helpless, just standing here, watching that boat...."

"No," Renie countered. "We are not helpless! I think I know how we can stop them!"

Twila gasped in alarm as Renie pulled her arm and hailed a passing taxi. "We haven't got much time! We'll have to hurry!"

13

THE OPEN SPEEDBOAT hugged the coastline; it was racing northward, a large fishtail hanging off one side and an inflated rubber crocodile poking its long nose off the stern. In the distance, on the darker water of the open sea, the clumsy fishing cruiser moved slowly up the coast in the direction of the unnamed cove.

Renie turned off the speedboat's engine. "Okay. We're well ahead of them, Twila. Let's see how fast we can get me into costume."

They had done it so many times that the operation was smooth, even in the confines of the boat. "What if they swerve away from the mouth of the cove?" Twila worried.

"Why would they? They're following the coast all the way, like I knew they would. They're not on a pleasure cruise, Twila. They have to be rendezvousing with somebody near one of the marinas."

She wriggled slowly into the costume, which was still wet around the waist from the afternoon of filming.

Twila urged the scaly suit carefully over Renie's hips. "What do you think are the chances of the harbor patrol listening to Edwin Noble?"

"I don't know. Edwin speaks fluent French, which ought to help. What I'm afraid of is that if a patrol boat does start out there, his captors will kill Dave rather than surrender him."

Twila cringed. "You realize, I hope, that we're insane to get in the middle of it?"

"Of course I realize it. Desperation spawns insanity. If Dave dies, how could we ever forgive ourselves for not trying to help? Besides, the gods of luck have been with us so far. Look how fast we were able to get out here."

"The gods of luck are fickle. Our luck is due to talent—our extraordinary coordination."

"Yes. And to Edwin's help."

"Yeah. Edwin was good. And we were. I didn't know how good we were in a crisis, Auntie Ren."

"We are good! But the worst is yet to come. We'd better keep faith in those gods of luck. This is really chancy."

Edwin had been at his concession, closing up, when they'd gone racing back to the film set. The watchman at the gate, recognizing Renie, had agreed to unlock the door of the costume room while Edwin pulled his van up to the gate. Traffic was light. The drive back to the marina had taken less than three minutes.

Renie, who by now knew all the harbor personnel, quickly arranged for the use of the speedboat, while Twila rushed to the *Sandrine II* at its permanent slip on the main pier for her swimsuit, her crocodile and her gun. And Edwin Noble had gone off, scratching his head in confusion, toward the office of the harbormaster to report dire trouble on the high seas.

"You're the one I'm worried about," Renie said, removing her bra and tossing it onto the heap of her clothes. "You must wear a life jacket."

"I can manage fine with my crocodile! A life jacket would slow me down. I and my faithful croc can make good time."

"It's open sea, Twila. I won't have you risk—"

"Don't argue! I'm letting you take the risk of getting shot, aren't I? I don't intend to disembark my crocodile on the open sea, damn it! Not till I have the boat rail to hang on to. Give me credit for being smart enough not to drown myself."

"What are you going to do if they don't kill the motor?"

"I think I can still get aboard the stern ladder. That boat is as slow as molasses. Believe me, they'll slow to a stop once they get opposite the islet. We can depend absolutely on that. No matter how desperate those guys think they are—they'll stop!"

Renie nodded and made the last adjustments to her costume while Twila moved up to take over the wheel. "Thank heaven the boat has a diver's ladder. I just hope Dave is all right." She was grateful beyond words for Twila's bravery and grit and for her love of adventure, which had propelled her into the middle of Renie's crazy scheme with little thought for its craziness.

They did not try to converse over the roar of the motor. Twila steered the shallow boat at high speed, along the shoreline, following the curve that dipped to form the basin-shaped cove. Beyond, the cruiser was chugging along, still some distance from the cove's mouth. The nearest islet was almost directly in its path.

Twila and her crocodile disembarked on that islet. Renie steered to the nearest coastal rocks, quickly tied up the boat out of sight and dived into the water. Propelled by her caudal fin, she reached the islet with time to spare before the cruiser moved into close range.

Behind them the sky was turning orange. The very first shadows of twilight were darkening the waves. The shadows were good; they would provide a cover for Twila while she and the faithful croc bounced over the water.

Renie fearfully touched the gun strapped to the top of the crocodile's head. "Don't use this unless you absolutely have to. Give it to Dave. Let him use it, not you. Promise, Twila."

"You seem to think I can't. It's my gun. I've fired it lots of times."

"Not at people! Twila, promise. Only if you *have* to."

"Okay. Okay, I promise. If they see me, though, they're dead men."

"Oh, God," Renie said. "I'm so scared."

Twila hugged her. "So am I. My adrenaline has never pumped like this. We'll do this. We're just crazy enough to do this!" She ducked low on the rock; the boat was getting closer, so close that they could see two men on deck, one in the wheelhouse and another at the railing. Dave was not one of them.

Renie prayed he was still alive.

BELOW, in the cabin of the cruiser, Dave was handcuffed to a solid oak railing. His head was throbbing both from anger and the cut on his temple that had not stopped bleeding. Tristan had warned him to leave the Mediterranean coast. He hadn't moved fast enough.

Someone must have spotted him, or perhaps, as Tristan had said once, the authorities had investigated every person who died in the crash as a matter of routine. Who had first learned he was still alive he could not guess. Terrorist groups had ways of following investigations that involved their deeds. With spies lurking everywhere, the police information had obviously spread like a match touched to dry timber, probably in a matter of hours.

He tugged at the handcuff that held him. On a cluttered counter a few feet away lay a toolbox. His freedom was inside that box—a screwdriver. His captors hadn't noticed when they cuffed him to the railing that it had a seam held by screws on the underside. With a few turns of a screwdriver, he could separate the railing and slide the handcuff off the wooden bar.

The toolbox was out of reach. He could stretch his free hand to within a few inches of it, but a few inches were no better than a few feet. He was held fast.

He heard the cruiser's engine sputter and stop. It made no sense to stop this soon, on the open sea, unless they planned to kill him and dump his body overboard. That was probably the plan. He waited, barely breathing. But there were no footsteps on the stairs. Why had they stopped?

Peering out of the square porthole, Dave saw the reason. Sitting on the nearest islet of the unnamed cove, just a few degrees off the port bow, was a mermaid. The orange sky was at her back, gleaming on the iridescent scales of her tail. Her hair was wet on her shoulders, her breasts were exposed. She was holding a mirror, using it to catch the reflections of the sun, probably to bring attention to herself.

"Renie, my God!" he breathed, gripping the ledge until his knuckles turned white.

He could hear the startled voices of the men on deck above him. *How the bloody hell could she do this?*

His eyes caught sight of something green and silver bobbing up and down in the water, hitting against the hull. He turned his head to see it better.

Twila's crocodile.

Twila's inflatable crocodile, grinning from the water like a sea monster.

His head swam with fear and confusion. What in the name of sanity were Renie and Twila up to? Whatever it was could get them killed!

The hatch door creaked open. Twila appeared in silhouette against the light. Lithe as a cat, dripping wet in her bikini, she moved down the steps and was at his side before he caught a breath.

"You're alive!" she whispered.

"Twila, what crazy—?"

She was flustered. "I had a gun, but I dropped it in the water, trying to get up on deck. Those two gawking fools are leaning over the rail, looking at Renie and going completely bananas. I crawled right behind them. King Kong could have crawled behind them!"

Dave felt himself begin to sweat. "Get a screwdriver out of that toolbox."

Her eyebrows shot up, but she obeyed without question and stood by, watching him unscrew the seam of the railing with his free hand, until he could slip the cuff off the oak bar.

"What are you going to do?" she whispered desperately. "Do they have guns?"

"They have guns, but I have the advantage of surprise."

He rummaged through a galley drawer and found a knife, not a very large one, but better than nothing.

"Stay in the hatchway, Twila. Don't come up unless I get overpowered or killed. If I do, then get off the boat as fast as you can."

"I can't swim, remember?"

He swore an oath under his breath. "Grab a life jacket from the cockpit and get the hell off, if it comes to that!"

"I could help you...."

"These men are murderers. Don't come up, Twila. Don't."

He turned, opened the hatch door and stuck his head up.

The boat was bobbing on the water with no one at the helm. Just as Dave emerged from the cabin, one of the men turned and headed toward the wheelhouse, probably intending to start the engine and steer closer to the mermaid. Very possibly to try to capture her. Dave took the man by surprise, hitting him so hard across the jaw that he fell backward against the rail, cracking several ribs and knocking the wind out of himself.

The second man, the one with the missing fingers, whirled around. Dave flashed the little knife. When the terrorist dived toward him, Dave dropped the knife and slammed his fist into the attacker's cheek. He followed up with another blow, in which the steel handcuff, still fastened to Dave's left wrist, caught his enemy in the mouth.

The villain, stunned, struggled to pull a gun from his belt, but Dave was too fast. He grabbed the man's wrist, forcing him to drop the gun. Dave recovered the weapon while the second terrorist was still writhing in pain on the deck, holding his sides.

It was over that soon.

"Twila!" Dave said, panting. "See if that bloke on deck has a gun under his coat. Do it carefully."

She pulled it out triumphantly. The man, standing with upraised hands, his mouth bleeding, was pointing wildly toward the islet, mumbling incoherently in broken English about a mermaid. Dave was unable to identify his accent.

"Boy, can you fight!" Twila raved, moving to Dave's side, keeping his gun aimed at the moaning man. "You just took out two guys!"

"Two very distracted guys," he said, still struggling to catch his breath.

"What do we do now?"

"We return to Savenay."

"The police didn't believe us when we tried to tell them you were kidnapped." She looked at him. "These *are* bad guys, right, Dave?"

"Very bad guys," he said and smiled. With his sleeve he wiped perspiration from his face. The cut was bleeding again.

"Are you okay?" she asked.

"Never better." He motioned to his captive to move into the wheelhouse, while Twila kept her gun aimed at the writhing one. "Renie must have a boat nearby. Does she? Can she get back okay?"

"Yes. Renie's fine."

Dave was preparing to start the engine when he saw the flashing red, green and white lights of the coastal police heading toward them at breakneck speed.

"Yowee!" Twila yelled. "Your good buddy Edwin got their attention!"

Two minutes later four uniformed officers boarded the cruiser. They found one man moaning on deck, another with his arms high in the air, gazing glassy-eyed across the port rail toward the unnamed cove. They found a shivering woman in a bikini with a gun in each hand, aiming both barrels at her captives.

No one else was there.

Dave swam fast in the undulating shadows of the sea surface.

Suddenly she was there, as if she had risen from the World of the Waves.

She grasped his hand tightly. He was out of breath and a little dizzy. He reached out to touch her lips with his fingertips.

"You're bleeding," she said. "Are you all right?"

"Just short of breath," he panted. "My clothes are weighing me down."

Renie dived under, unbuttoned his jeans, pulled them off and let them float away. He had kicked off his shoes on deck. "Can you make it to shore?"

"I can make it to our cave, if you'll stay with me. They won't find us there." He struggled out of his water-logged sweatshirt, tugging hard as one sleeve caught on the handcuff. He didn't have enough breath to say any more as they headed toward the shore, but he was a strong swimmer, used to distances in currents much stronger and surf much heavier than those of this quiet Riviera cove.

Once behind the concealing rocks, Renie flopped onto the white sand in front of the cave opening.

He stretched out beside her, breathing hard.

She touched his temple. "You're hurt."

"I'm all right."

She examined his wrist, which was bruised blue from struggling against the steel restraint. "You're still handcuffed."

He closed his eyes and lay for a time in silence, gathering his strength. Then he sat up, took her into his arms and held her tightly. "Have you any idea what you did tonight? You and Twila saved my life."

Renie smiled happily. "I knew she could do it! I didn't hear any gunshots. I was so afraid she'd shoot somebody."

"She lost her gun in the water. She saved me with a screwdriver."

"What?"

"Never mind now. I'd rather not talk about it now. You'll get every detail from her later, probably a hundred times. Twila is fine. She's a heroine. She just captured the two most wanted terrorists in the world."

"What?" she repeated.

He did not answer, but simply held her, feeling the beating of her heart. Then he said, "And you, my love. Casting your magic spell. Those terrorists were so mesmerized I could have pitched them overboard with one toe. But why did you do it? If the police thought they were government agents, why didn't you?"

"They were the goblins," Renie answered. "When they were shoving you into the car, I saw his hand. It was the hand of the goblin Fireskog. That's when I knew."

"I don't believe it!"

"He is Fireskog, isn't he? Fireskog and Grig. They were. They had to be." She shivered in his arms. "Dave, I was so scared. I was afraid they would kill you."

"They would have."

He kissed her deeply.

Reluctantly she pulled away. "Does this mean you're not going to leave me?"

"I'll never leave you." He brushed her wet hair from her cheek. "When I looked out the porthole and saw you on the islet...it was like the first time I saw you...your beauty overwhelmed me. But this time you weren't an illusion. You were the woman I love and you were in terrible danger because of loving me. I've never known what it is to be loved so much." He held her close and whispered, "No, I'll never leave you."

He felt the warmth of her tears against his face and bent to kiss them away. "You understand, I'll have to go to London to straighten out some details of my...life. But I'll come back to you as soon as I can."

"And...the cameras?" she asked, barely breathing.

"The cameras no longer matter. I'm free now. And alive, thanks to you."

She hugged him tightly and laughed through her tears. Her tail flapped restlessly against the sand. "Oh,

Dave, get me out of this damned thing. I can't bear this restraint now, here...."

He knew how to do it this time and pulled gently at the costume to release her.

She said, "I have clothes in the boat, not very far from here."

"I'll get them for you."

"No, never mind right now. Just hold me. Keep me warm and tell me you were joking about the most wanted terrorists in the world."

"No. They really are."

"But how? How did you get mixed up with them?"

"It's a long story."

"Then just hit the highlights, but tell me. I'm so tired of guessing who you really are, Dave."

He lay back and looked up at her... at her body, silhouetted against the gray-pink sky... her long, golden hair, falling damp over her shoulders, catching the light of sunset... her blue eyes, filled with misty love....

He reached up and urged her gently to him so that her head rested on his chest and his arm fitted around her. He sighed heavily, then smiled and said, "One day, two years ago, a weird thing happened on my way to catch a plane...."

Epilogue

DAVE MET RENIE at the Nice airport with a kiss and a bouquet of long-stemmed roses, twelve red and a thirteenth—one yellow rose in the center—a symbol of his lonesome heart, he said.

"Renie, it's been the longest three months of my life!"

She hugged him, trying not to crush the roses. "The past three weeks have been the worst. Not a word from you, except that cablegram, saying you'd meet me today! Where on earth have you *been?*"

"Africa," he said. "Zimbabwe and Zambia and Malawi."

"Really? What were you doing? Looking at African art?"

"African sculpture. And I wasn't just looking, I was buying." He squeezed her hand and led her in the direction of the baggage-claim area. "When is Twila coming?"

"Tomorrow. Twila got off in Paris to shop. It's all she could talk about. She tried to coax me to join her, but I couldn't bear to wait another day to see you. I thought that film was *never* going to get finished."

"Is it a good film?" he asked.

"I don't know. I haven't seen it. The editing isn't even finished. I hope it's a good film, Dave. I don't see how it could not be."

While they waited hand in hand for her bags, she asked him, "How did you get the divorce so fast?"

He smiled. "I didn't have to. She married again when I was officially dead. After requests from both our solicitors, the court ruled that her second marriage was legal, which meant the first was automatically dissolved."

Later, driving from the airport, Dave said, "We're going to stay in Nice tonight."

"I guess we should, since Twila is arriving tomorrow afternoon."

"We would stay in Nice regardless of Twila's arrival. There is something here I must show you."

He seemed acquainted with the city as he drove. The traffic was heavy and noisy, but the chaos appeared to be of no concern to Dave. He navigated like a Frenchman, pulling in and out of the traffic with one narrow miss after another.

As they headed steadily east, soon Renie could feel the ocean air again.

"The port is out there," Dave said. "And the Old Town. You'll like the Old Town. At least, I hope you'll like it. I've leased a small shop there. I'm going into the import business again."

Renie felt a rush of excitement, partly his excitement, partly her own. "A shop? That's what you wanted to show me?"

"And more. There's an apartment above it, where we can stay when we're in Nice. It's not furnished yet, but we can make it splendid with some money and imagination."

"We're moving here?"

"No, I'll engage someone to work the shop. We'll be here some of the time."

He made his way through the narrow, twisting streets, finally parked, and led her down steps and around a curve. They were on a short street, lined with small shops and restaurants. Above them loomed the old castle hill, where once a fortress had stood.

"It's really charming," Renie said.

"We'll walk up that hill later. The view from the top is a stunner. And here . . . a fish market is held in the square in the mornings. . . ." He stopped before a small, ocher-colored shop with glass windows and a carved door. "This is it. You can see how many tourists are attracted to this area. I was lucky to find such a good spot."

The inside was empty, except for wooden crates piled in the back room. Dave opened one of the crates, rummaged through packing material and lifted out a sculpture of a bird in green soapstone.

"It's from the Shona tribe," he said. "They believe the spirits of the dead come alive again as birds. The history of these bird sculptures goes all the way back to the medieval kingdom of Munhumutapa. Here . . . you'll love the feel of it."

She ran her fingers over the stone. "I know nothing of the people or the places you speak of."

"Do you want to see them? Would you like to travel to Africa with me?"

"I'd love it! Will we?"

"Yes. When you're not involved in films...."

Renie set down the sculpture. "I'm not going to make any more films. The mermaid project was fun and important to me. But I've never been interested in acting and not that good at it. And the life-style of an actress doesn't appeal to me. I'm just not the type. I made a lot of money, and the experience was great. But it's over, Dave. I much prefer your kind of life."

He pulled her into her arms and swung her around. "You're all mine? That's the best news I've ever heard! Now we're really going to celebrate!"

He took her hand. "I'll show you the upstairs apartment. Be warned, it's not large, and there isn't anything in it except a bed. A bed and three chilled bottles of excellent French champagne. Remember, Renie? How good champagne is for celebrating?"

THE BELL IN THE STEEPLE of the Cauvier village church began to ring as Renie and Dave stepped out of the chapel into bright sunshine. She wore a white dress of heavy Belgian lace and carried a bouquet of white roses.

Behind them followed Twila and Edwin Noble, she in burgundy velvet, carrying red roses. "Look at us, Auntie Ren!" she had howled that morning. "Snow White and Rose Red!" A group of smiling wedding guests formed a circle around them as they stepped under a nearby shade tree.

The waiting musicians began to play.

Dave took his bride into his arms. "Our dance, Mrs. Collister."

With the small circle of guests clapping and the church bell ringing, the bride and groom danced their first dance together in the sunshine of the ancient village square.

Brew: He'd fought his way off the streets . . . but his past threatened the woman he loved.

THE BAD BOY
by Roseanne Williams
Temptation #401, July 1992

All men are not created equal. Some are rough around the edges. Tough-minded but tenderhearted. Incredibly sexy. The tempting fulfillment of every woman's fantasy.

When it's time to fight for what they believe in, to win that special woman, our Rebels and Rogues are heroes at heart. Twelve Rebels and Rogues, one each month in 1992, only from Harlequin Temptation. Don't miss the upcoming books by our fabulous authors such as JoAnn Ross, Ruth Jean Dale and Janice Kaiser.

OVER THE YEARS, TELEVISION HAS BROUGHT
THE LIVES AND LOVES OF MANY CHARACTERS INTO
YOUR HOMES. NOW HARLEQUIN INTRODUCES YOU
TO THE TOWN AND PEOPLE OF

One small town—twelve terrific love stories.

GREAT READING... GREAT SAVINGS...
AND A FABULOUS FREE GIFT!

Each book set in Tyler is a self-contained love story; together, the
twelve novels stitch the fabric of the community.

By collecting proofs-of-purchase found in each Tyler book, you can
receive a fabulous gift, ABSOLUTELY FREE! And use our special
Tyler coupons to save on your next TYLER book purchase.

Join us for the fifth TYLER book,
BLAZING STAR by Suzanne Ellison, available in July.

Is there really a murder cover-up?
Will Brick and Karen overcome differences and find true love?

Summer Reading
At Its Best

In July, Harlequin and Silhouette bring readers the Big Summer Read Program. Heat up your summer with these four exciting new novels by top Harlequin and Silhouette authors.

SOMEWHERE IN TIME by Barbara Bretton
YESTERDAY COMES TOMORROW by Rebecca Flanders
A DAY IN APRIL by Mary Lynn Baxter
LOVE CHILD by Patricia Coughlin

From time travel to fame and fortune, this program offers something for everyone.

Available at your favorite retail outlet.

BSR

FREE GIFT OFFER

To receive your free gift, send us the specified number of proofs-of-purchase from any specially marked Free Gift Offer Harlequin or Silhouette book with the Free Gift Certificate properly completed, plus a check or money order (do not send cash) to cover postage and handling payable to Harlequin/Silhouette Free Gift Promotion Offer. We will send you the specified gift.

FREE GIFT CERTIFICATE

ITEM	A. GOLD TONE EARRINGS	B. GOLD TONE BRACELET	C. GOLD TONE NECKLACE
# of proofs-of-purchase required	3	6	9
Postage and Handling	$1.75	$2.25	$2.75
Check one	☐	☐	☐

Name: _____

Address: _____

City: _____ State: _____ Zip Code: _____

Mail this certificate, specified number of proofs-of-purchase and a check or money order for postage and handling to: HARLEQUIN/SILHOUETTE FREE GIFT OFFER 1992, P.O. Box 9057, Buffalo, NY 14269-9057. Requests must be received by July 31, 1992.

PLUS—Every time you submit a completed certificate with the correct number of proofs-of-purchase, you are automatically entered in our MILLION DOLLAR SWEEPSTAKES! No purchase or obligation necessary to enter. See below for alternate means of entry and how to obtain complete sweepstakes rules.

MILLION DOLLAR SWEEPSTAKES
NO PURCHASE OR OBLIGATION NECESSARY TO ENTER

To enter, hand-print (mechanical reproductions are not acceptable) your name and address on a 3″×5″ card and mail to Million Dollar Sweepstakes 6097, c/o either P.O. Box 9056, Buffalo, NY 14269-9056 or P.O. Box 621, Fort Erie, Ontario L2A 5X3. Limit: one entry per envelope. Entries must be sent via 1st-class mail. For eligibility, entries must be received no later than March 31, 1994. No liability is assumed for printing errors, lost, late or misdirected entries.

Sweepstakes is open to persons 18 years of age or older. All applicable laws and regulations apply. Sweepstakes offer void wherever prohibited by law. Prizewinners will be determined no later than May 1994. Chances of winning are determined by the number of entries distributed and received. For a copy of the Official Rules governing this sweepstakes offer, send a self-addressed, stamped envelope (WA residents need not affix return postage) to: Million Dollar Sweepstakes Rules, P.O. Box 4733, Blair, NE 68009.

✂ HT3U

ONE PROOF-OF-PURCHASE
To collect your fabulous FREE GIFT you must include the necessary FREE GIFT proofs-of-purchase with a properly completed offer certificate.

(See inside back cover for offer details)